LONGSHOT HYPOTHESIS

SHADOW OF THE DOMINION: BOOK 1

BLAZE WARD

KNOTTED ROAD PRESS

Longshot Hypothesis
Shadow of the Dominion: Book 1
Blaze Ward
Copyright © 2019 Blaze Ward
All rights reserved
Published by Knotted Road Press
www.KnottedRoadPress.com

ISBN: 978-1-64470-069-3

Cover art:

ID 102507544 © Luca Olestri | Dreamstime.com

Never miss a release!
If you'd like to be notified of new releases, sign up for my newsletter.

I will never spam you, or use your email for nefarious purposes. You can also unsubscribe at any time.

http://www.blazeward.com/newsletter/

Shadow of the Dominion

Longshot Hypothesis

Hard Bargain

Outermost

Dominion-427

Phoenix

Princess Rualoh

The Jessica Keller Chronicles

Auberon

Queen of the Pirates

Last of the Immortals

Goddess of War

Flight of the Blackbird

The Red Admiral

St. Legier

Winterhome

Petron

CS-405

Queen Anne's Revenge

Packmule

Persephone

Additional Alexandria Station Stories

The Story Road

Siren

Two Bottles of Wine with a War God

The Science Officer Series

The Science Officer

The Mind Field

The Gilded Cage

The Pleasure Dome

The Doomsday Vault

The Last Flagship

The Hammerfield Gambit

The Hammerfield Payoff

Earth Force Sky Patrol

Birth of the Star Dragon

Flight of the Star Dragon

Call of the Star Dragon

Shadow of the Star Dragon

Trial of the Star Dragon

Other Science Fiction Stories

Myrmidons

Moonshot

Menelaus

Earthquake Gun

Moscow Gold

[1]

VALENTINIAN

IT STARTED IN A BAR.

Didn't it always? Exciting things in space never began in a station library or a barber shop, although Valentinian wasn't about to say that too loud, even in his own head. Tempting the gods, and all that.

Valentinian had never really been a reader type so he hadn't ever spent that much time in libraries. Still, that always struck him as the far end of places from a bar, when it came to thinking up dumb ideas. Starting an adventure in a library, as it were.

Best not to push his luck too far, ya know?

Coming to this station had been a dumb idea, but what was he, if not a living example of bad decisions in life?

How many other people had managed to get themselves kicked out of the Gymnasia Dominia? He had heard somewhere that more than ninety thousand applicants filed paperwork each year, for one thousand slots for students. Sure, half those would wash out in the next three years before they became officers in the Dominion Armada, but Valentinian hadn't exactly washed out.

Been kicked to the curb, more or less. The one guy they could pin it all on, when he'd only been *one* of the ringleaders. Can't have the kids of important people sullied by scandal now, can we? Oh, heavens no.

Valentinian nursed the drink in his hands, scanned the rich and important people around him, and tried not to snarl too loud or dwell on the distant past. Well, three years. Twenty years old and he had thought he had it made. Top quarter of his second-year class on grades and points. Gonna be a star.

Nobody had counted on the White Hats, the Dominion's Internal Security Bureau, suddenly getting involved. It had only been a little contraband, nothing even illegal on about half the planets of the Dominion.

But enough to open a space in the roster when he got frog-marched out the side door and tossed into the metaphorical street on his ass.

Valentinian suppressed the growl.

Coming here had been a bad idea. Not just this bar, but this system, let alone this station. Normally, he would have said you couldn't pay him enough to come to Dominion Prime, the so-called Winter Palace Orbital Station of the Dominator himself. Security checks at damned near every frame and hatch. Places off-limits to everyone most of the time.

But yeah, he'd apparently been lying about no price being enough. Someone had offered him a stupid amount of money to come here. To pick up a cargo, well, whatever you called it. A charter, he supposed. The contract had been stupidly long, but Valentinian had always had a head for legal mumbo-jumbo and esoteric accounting.

Had gotten him into *Gymnasia*. And probably gotten him kicked out, too, one of those times when the dice rolls just fell the wrong way when he had already pushed his luck too far.

He still didn't know, three years later, where his scams had fallen apart. Didn't really matter. Just being here, smelling the scent of these people, brought it all back to the surface.

He took another tiny sip and kept his face calm.

Being around the beautiful people had him grouchy. And he missed Artaxerxes.

His now-former first mate had been, was, *would always be* a doughy, goofy, engineering-type. And probably more than twice Valentinian's age. Into his fifth decade, anyway, although the man never really talked about it. Beard all gray coming in now and wrinkles etching themselves into that laughing forehead.

Artaxerxes had gone and found himself a woman. Worse, a woman who owned a bar and had decided to marry herself a partner. Bed or business was a little fuzzy, but Valentinian hadn't seen the marriage contract. Didn't really care *that* much.

It had been enough that the man had packed his few belongings at Tuska Station and departed with a skip in his step.

Normally, Valentinian would have remained on Tuska Station for longer than a day, looking for his next cargo run somewhere, and doing more than putting up a couple of help-wanted posters, but a chandler had gotten in touch with him. Had a contract for Valentinian, was he interested? Total stranger personally, but the man had good reviews on the public boards and no major lawsuits that Valentinian had been able to find in the records.

Not that that mattered as much in the Dominion as other nations, like Qetesh or Lei-Zu. Even beyond those in

Wildspace you weren't going to find anyone as militantly crazy as the Dominion.

Nobody was.

A caste of warrior monks dedicated to the military arts and surrounded by nervous neighbors. A meritocracy in the hardest sense, where your birth would only get you as far as your family might lift you, with the understanding that your screw-ups might bring them down as well, so nobody was going to do you favors that didn't make them look good in the process.

A place where a kid from the wrong side of the tracks, with the right kind of mind, could score a place at Gymnasia on his brains, since he was nothing like those blade-fighting lunatics. At least until the day he screwed up and didn't have the sorts of family support network his unindicted co-conspirators had been able to hide behind, when it came time to sweep it all under the rug and find a scapegoat.

But he was here. Dominion Prime itself, don't you know. With the promise of a contract paying way too much cash for something as simple as a straight charter.

Valentinian didn't believe for a moment the story that his ship, the *Longshot Hypothesis*, was exactly the perfect one to hire for six months.

For one thing, the ship was a cargo transport that had been modified to have a half-dozen cabins for paying customers, not a dedicated pleasure yacht. And the contract specified that he would be hauling nearly twenty people, so that upper deck would be crammed full and then some.

Granted, the semi-famous girl-band/dance troupe Solaria Femina had nine members these days, all ethnically and physically identical girls aged sixteen to twenty-two, answering to the woman in charge, plus a Dancemaster, a Songmaster, and a Chastitymaster, whatever the hell that was. Throw in a couple of costumers. And we can't forget the a Nutritionist, however nice it would be, since part of the contract involved them bringing their own food aboard and feeding his crew. If he had one beyond himself at that point.

Working on that.

Valentinian had almost talked himself out of the contract, in spite of the money he would make, but somehow just couldn't let that kind of cash go by the wayside. His profit margin after operating costs alone after six months would cover him for at least two years of pure goofing off afterwards, if he wanted.

Not that he would. Every single spare Solar would go into a series of investment accounts, mostly in Laurentia or Lei-Zu. Never places where the good folks of the Dominion who had screwed him so bad already could get at it easily.

Brains and luck only got you so far. And Valentinian had learned the value of hustle. It had gotten him back on his feet after the fuck up. Had gotten him into a crooked card game where he wasn't the mark, and could score enough collateral damage on the final few hands to buy himself a broken-down, *vintage* cargo transport.

The good ship *Longshot Hypothesis*. Because him being any kind of success at that point in his life had only been that, a longshot hypothesis.

But luck and hustle also found him Artaxerxes as a crew to help get it into pretty decent shape. Gave him a future.

Gotta save funds at all times.

Even this drink cost more than he would have spent, normally, but he was waiting for the woman who represented *Solaria Femina* to arrive with executed contracts that had been filed with the authorities.

The Dominator, leader of the Dominion, might be a crazed berserker intent on taking over the universe, but the government itself was run by the Solar Party, and they were all about legal contracts. Maybe the only way to keep the warriors in check.

A Dude walked into the bar and almost everybody at least glanced over at him. Noise didn't stop, but it hiccupped, even with the jaded denizens of a high-class joint like this. Nobody came to Dominion Prime without a reason, and a lot of Solars in their pockets.

And this dude looked like trouble.

Big man, just a little shy of two meters tall. Broad shoulders. Intense face.

Valentinian had a good view of the guy, as he was facing the door with his back tucked into a booth in the corner. Monster. Valentinian was a little over average height and had acquired a few muscles from moving pallets and boxes around.

Stranger had half a head on him. And muscles on muscles. Like maybe he could bend nails with his fingers.

Older. Maybe fifty. Blond hair cut short enough to start to show the gray hairs through. Clean shaven, with a jaw that would probably make women swoon.

Valentinian was expecting blue eyes when the guy locked on him across the bar. That was the most common genotype among the warrior nobility of the Dominion. Not dark-haired and dark-eyed exotics like Valentinian was.

Instead, eyes like molten bronze focused this way. Valentinian suddenly regretted ever setting foot on this station. Tuska, or other places, and he would have a shock pistol on his hip, everywhere he went. Didn't prevent ruckus, but sure tamped it down a lot when people wanted to get out of hand.

But nobody was allowed to be armed around here except the Solar Guard. And maybe any White Hats he ran into.

This would have been a good time to have a weapon.

Dude looked serious about whatever was crossing his mind. Troublesome serious.

Staring at Valentinian.

And walking this way.

Crap.

Valentinian considered the booth. He should have picked a standing table to wait. That would have at least given him something to knock over at the guy, but this booth was attached to the floor and wall, and somehow, he didn't think a face full of cheap whiskey would do much more than just piss that monster off.

Hopefully, one of the bartenders or waitstaff had their hands near a panic button right about now. Bad day to get your ass kicked.

Monster got closer. He was wearing baggy gray pants tucked into tall, leather boots. Blue tunic, belted and long sleeved, was half-hidden under a light jacket in the same gray fabric as the pants. It was the kind of outfit you wore shipside when you left the heater down a few degrees or so to save money. Like Valentinian routinely did.

Rough hands. Gnarled and scarred, like the man had done decades of work with his hands in rough circumstances, except his face didn't have the matching battering Valentinian would have expected.

The man did have a scar on his face. Faint enough to be almost invisible, so old.

Started just inside the hairline on his left forehead and came inward on the cheek diagonally, just missing the eye and fading before it got to his beard. Only thing Valentinian could think of that made a cut that straight and that clean would be blade-fighting, the kind you did without sparring armor. What the craziest of the craziest warrior monks of the Dominion did to prove they were tougher, meaner, *better* than everyone else.

What the hell did I do to warrant this guy's attention?

The man stopped about a body length away. Somehow, Valentinian knew it was the proper distance to greet someone, just before combat broke out on the training floor.

"Valentinian Tarasicodissa?" he asked.

Man had a rich voice. Baritone. Sure of himself. Hard as nails.

Probably mean as a hungry snake, too.

"That's right," Valentinian replied with the faintest nod. No point denying it or trying to weasel his way out of whatever trap he had stepped into this time.

He would have liked to see if the bartender was calling for help, but taking his eyes off the stranger sounded like a bad idea. Not that he could have done something to prevent getting his ass kicked by this stranger, but Valentinian still wanted to see it coming.

Dude reached a hand inside his jacket and pulled out something as Valentinian tensed. Looked like a wad of paper, folded over a couple of times and kinda mashed into a pocket too small.

The man pulled it more or less flat and stepped close enough to place it on the tabletop in front of Valentinian, leaving him no choice but to take his eyes off the stranger and see what it was.

HELP WANTED. FIRST MATE POSITION.

Shit.

I put that up at Tuska Station. And a couple here when I landed.

Valentinian looked up at the monstrously-huge man towering over him. The man did not look anything like an engineer. Not that Valentinian really needed one. He could do most of the technical work himself by now, after Artaxerxes had taught him the right systems.

Maybe a pretty good stevedore, with all those muscles.

"You know how to tune a solar engine?" Valentinian asked pointedly.

Might as well cut to the chase. Anything to get rid of trouble like this.

"When I was about your age," the man answered with the faintest hint of a gleam in those bronze-colored eyes. "Not since, but I figure I can pick it up again. Got more experience programming them."

"Job doesn't pay much," Valentinian offered, hoping something would drive the man off.

Being a tramp freighter crewman on a starship always sounded way more alluring and rewarding than the squalid realities of broken life-support fans, bribes at stations to not get roughed up by local hoodlums, or the monotonous boredom of travel between stars.

"Got some money saved up," the man replied easily. "Really looking for something different in my life."

Oh, goody. Mid-life crisis has hit and dude wants to grow his hair long and hang out with babes, rather than deal with a shrill harpy of a wife and kids he doesn't know. Isn't that the Dominion Dream?

"Warrants in any systems?" Valentinian pressed, hoping to find a lever on the man. Anything. "Prior convictions or powerful enemies I should know about?"

"No warrants," the man's shoulders came down and back. "No convictions. No enemies I know about, but I'm sure there are people out there looking to do me wrong for something I've forgotten about by now."

Valentinian was about to ask for paperwork he could use to look the man up, when a small commotion at the door distracted him.

The pictures did not do the woman justice. Any of them.

Tall and elegantly thin, she looked like she had been built

out of anger and barbed wire then covered over with expensive beauty cream and mascara.

Slightly-oversized chest was mushed up in a royal blue top a little too tight, but he doubted that was an oversight on her part. Focused the eyes on the center of her body rather than her face. Tight waist below that just emphasized amazing hips as well.

She spotted him and started to cross the bar, clacking on high heels as most of the eyes in the place followed her. Like you could miss the waves of frustrated anger radiating off the woman like a short-range sensor probe.

Lianearia Cleray. The woman in charge of Solaria Femina.

Valentinian had looked her up and gone pretty damned deep when the first contract request came through. She had been with that very first batch of girls, when some music mogul put together a girl-band dance troupe, nearly twenty years ago. The list of ex-members who had been chewed up and spit out since then was amazingly long, but few ever lasted until they were even twenty-two.

Somehow, this woman had clawed her way back in years later, on the business side of things, until she was running it now, too old to be part of the in-crowd, at all of thirty-six, if the bio wasn't lying about her age.

Up close, lines and shadows out of place suggested some amazingly-expensive work on her face and neck, the parts not covered by the blue bodice and matching skirt.

Valentinian guessed her hair was naturally a mousy brown, based on her eyebrows, but the rest of her mane was a lush strawberry-blond that came down to her shoulders and framed her beauty.

She could stop traffic with that body on any planet or station he'd ever visited.

"There you are," she snapped as she came to a halt beside the tall stranger, her eyes locked on Valentinian.

The woman registered the giant next to her with a look of such calculated disdain that Valentinian was pretty sure he'd be rich, if he could figure out how to bottle and sell it on the black market.

"Go away," she commanded the giant in a shrill, waspy voice.

For the briefest moment, Valentinian saw a rage of immense depth appear in the giant's bronze eyes. Volcanic, in every sense of the word. Trouble.

The guy surprised him by silently nodding to Valentinian and bowing slightly to Madame Cleray. He withdrew to the bar, and Valentinian lost track of him as the woman stormed his booth and whistled loudly for a waitress.

"Cheval," she demanded.

Valentinian hoped that they didn't put the single most expensive brandy in the bar on his tab. That was the sort of thing that killed profit margins, and he didn't even know if he had a deal with the woman yet.

"Is your ship ready to load?" she demanded as the waitress left.

Gods, the woman was gorgeous. And that smell. Being this close just made it all the more obvious. That scent of something sharp and sweet and sexy emanated from her like chemical warfare agents. His brain noted that it was almost pheromonic in nature, and not just intense.

Not a woman who let any possible edge elude her.

He had wondered why the music industry hadn't given her a second career, after Solaria Femina was done with her, but those girls were supposed to be bubbleheaded bimbos who were interchangeable. Not sharks. Nothing like Cleray.

"It is," Valentinian answered simply.

"Good," she snapped.

The bodice apparently had a pocket across the front, almost like a kangaroo's pouch. She reached a hand inside and pulled out a thin sheet of plas-paper and slid it across the table to him.

Valentinian reached into a pocket on his jacket automatically and pulled out his card-reader, sliding the plas-paper into it and letting the system start chugging.

He already had a copy of the agreed-upon contract loaded, so now it just had to confirm that the signed and executed version was identical. And had all the right stamps and approvals from Dominion authorities on it.

Handshakes were nice, but contract law was serious business. You shook hands over a bar bet. When serious money was changing hands, you filed the paperwork with the Hall of Records first. Way safer after that if there were any misunderstandings that you couldn't settled before you were explaining things to a Dominion Magistrate.

The machine chirped happily a few seconds later.

He looked up to see her eyes hooded, the rage masked, at least for now.

"You have a reputation for integrity, Tarasicodissa," she announced in a low, compelling voice, eyes sharp and probing, like maybe she didn't believe it. "I'd hardly start off our relationship by trying to screw you over."

Which merely suggested she'd be trying to chisel corners later, and looking for scams and outs once she got tired of him.

Not that Valentinian was surprised. The woman was a cold-blooded predator. She might look beautiful, but a good deal of work had been done above her collarbones, although he supposed she probably had done the breasts as well.

It just wasn't as obvious, if she had.

It was the hands that gave her away. Claws tipped in blood-red and starting to show liver spots on the back. She had built a career and a business empire on beauty, and it was fading a little every day.

Valentinian nodded and held his peace as the waitress returned with a glass of liquid gold. At least by price.

"To business," she said, raising her glass in a toast.

Valentinian joined her. He wasn't about to drink the rest of his whiskey in one breath, even as she put the whole glass of brandy away.

He did make a note to never get into a drinking contest with the woman, if she could hold her alcohol like that. Good way to lose money. And days.

Maybe he could take her to Tuska Station, just once, and let her loose on the old farts there who thought they could handle their booze.

That might be fun to watch.

"Shall we?" she demanded, sliding to the edge of the booth.

Valentinian was a beat behind her as she rose, taking a moment to ogle her bottom and finish his whiskey after all. She must still work out and dance hard, to have an ass that nice.

He was pretty sure she was utterly poisonous, though. Burn you just by touching, like some weeds he had heard about on wilder parts of many planets. Valentinian generally never got farther away from civilization than the closest bar or chandlery to the starport, unless he had to.

And even that was iffy. Going places and having fun usually required money he would rather spend on getting his ship, *Longshot Hypothesis*, in better running order. Or saving for a rainy day.

But it was a stupendous ass. And the bodice showed off muscles in the woman's back as he stood up to his full height, staring just about at the back of her head. But he already knew she was wearing heels.

Madame Cleray stopped so suddenly that he almost plowed into her from behind, but Valentinian had spent enough time on spaceships to dance to one side safely.

He stopped, too, when he saw what had caught her eye.

There were six of them.

Valentinian thought that was overkill, but maybe they knew something about the woman that he didn't.

Five bruisers in black and one pudgy lawyer in a fancy suit. The kind that probably cost about what his ship's operating costs ran per month.

"Going somewhere, my dear?" the lawyer asked in a honey-smooth voice that still managed to sound like rusty bearings in a fan about to seize.

The five goons spread out a little. More than enough to block the wide doorway.

And of course a joint like this didn't have a bouncer on duty. Possibly a few off-duty naval officers that might be capable of handling one of these guys, but not all five, assuming they even found a reason to get involved.

Valentinian knew he should have never gotten out of his bunk this morning.

"Go away, Nash," Cleray sneered. "I'm not signing your contract. We're done. Find some other fool you can skim funds off of."

"My dear, I'm wounded at such accusations," the man, called Nash apparently, answered. "I wonder if I should file for a breach of contract. And maybe throw in slander as well. I've heard some of the things you've said about me."

"Truth is a perfect defense against libel, Nash," Cleray cat-called cheerfully. "Try it. I'd be happy to be deposed officially."

Valentinian noted how quiet the bar had gotten. Upper middle class folks apparently not used to the posturing and braggadocio he ran into regularly, down dockside.

He really missed his shock pistol about now.

"We'll just see about that, Lianearia," Nash snarled, gesturing at Valentinian. "I see you've found a new victim."

"Interesting choice of words," she said. "Especially coming from you."

"Did you already sign a contract with this woman, boy?" Nash asked. "About to lose your soul?"

He didn't take particular insult from the term. Nash looked to be in his sixties. Squishy and soft. Manicured nails. Dyed hair.

Instead Valentinian just grinned. It had been a pretty good contract, but Valentinian supposed that maybe these other two folks hadn't had as pleasant a negotiation about things.

"Yes, it looks like he has," Nash continued. "I suppose we'll just have to convince you to tear it up."

Nash took a step forward. His goons spread out even more, actively intimidating the political whores and flunkies that had picked the wrong afternoon for a drink.

Five on one sucked. He was likely to end up in medbay, if he didn't do whatever this butterball demanded. And somehow, that deal didn't sound as good as hauling a crew of nubile teenage girls all over the galaxy for six to twelve months.

The woman shifted her feet a little. Not much, but enough that Valentinian decided that maybe some of that dance training might have taken place on a dojo floor.

"Seriously, Nash?" Cleray taunted the man. "Physical violence in public? Not your style at all. And I'm a girl."

Low blow. Telling, too, considering the way the man's eyes turned red.

"Grab her," he demanded.

The goons moved.

All of them were big fellows. Valentinian's height, with a

bunch of extra weight. Not all of it was muscle, but these boys were bad bouncers, not ninjas. The first one stepped close and threw a punch.

It was slow, awkward, and his feet were in the wrong position, so obviously he'd never actually learned how to fight in a bar. It was a MOST useful skill to develop.

Valentinian ducked the haymaker and used the crouched leverage to drive a fist into a soft belly, the kind that was spilling over a belt.

Air rushed out of the man in a hurry. He collapsed around the fist as Valentinian side-stepped. The rest were coming.

The woman did know some combat skills, but that just meant she tried a stupid, head-high kick at the man trying to grab her instead of punching him square in the balls. There was no force behind it, so she pretty much just slapped him with her foot. And pissed him off.

And then the others were all over him.

Valentinian threw a fist and hit something before he got clocked pretty good. Not spiraling stars, but close.

Somebody grabbed his right arm before he could pull it back.

Somebody else tangled his left arm against his side and grappled.

Third guy punched him square in the face.

That brought out the stars, but the two goons with holds kept him upright when falling on the floor right now sounded like a good idea.

Big dude pulled back his fist for another go.

This was gonna suck.

And nothing.

The fist never landed.

Instead, the mild concussion inside Valentinian's head made time slow way down, like those really good action movies, where so much is happening that they slo-mo the fight sequence and spin the camera around a few times in a single, dramatic shot so you don't miss anything.

The fist was like the sun overhead, about to rain down pain, when somebody hooked the wrist.

Valentinian felt the camera operator pivot expertly, even as his own head never moved.

The big guy, the one looking for a job before Cleray chased him off, had stepped up and hooked his elbow around the other dude's wrist and stopped the punch in the middle of the sky like an eclipse.

With his left hand, big dude rabbit-punched the goon three times, so fast that at normal speed it might appear as a single blow.

Awesome.

Then he GRABBED THE GUY AND LIFTED HIM OFF THE GROUND.

Except it was a hip-pivot throw that landed the victim into the legs of the goon that had just grabbed Madame Cleray in a body hold. Knocked him down and staggered her.

Other two were just too slow to process. Or maybe they were moving at normal speed as Valentinian went into overdrive to watch.

Dude bent forward and drove a kick back like an angry horse into the man holding Valentinian's left side. And suddenly that guy was gone.

Poof, just like that.

Then big and mean pivoted the other direction with the momentum, turning into the bouncer holding Valentinian's right hand with an elbow slam ox blow to the head straight out of a movie or something.

Cows usually went down for the count when the guy

with the stun hammer hit them that hard. Bouncer wasn't a cow, but he wasn't still waking up for a while either.

One of the guys tangled around Madame Cleray's feet managed to stand up. Valentinian might have told him that was a really bad idea, but he didn't like these guys that much.

Monster dude took a step and it was like he was flying through the air, except he was moving big-ugly-booted-foot-first into the goon's chest, and kicked him hard enough to drive the guy into one of those tables that were apparently bolted to the deck so that it wouldn't fall over. Bouncer three (four? whoever?) dented the post. Post dented bouncer three.

Last guy seemed just about ready to find his wits and his feet, maybe even standing up when the big guy fell on his head fist first.

And down.

Big dude straightened back up and looked around. Smiled at Nash.

Total elapsed time, even flowing at the amazing speed of an action movie: maybe three seconds. Five guys down. Not just down. Out. Bye-bye.

Big guy's hair wasn't even mussed.

He took a step up to this Nash fellow and leaned down to get right into his face.

"Don't follow," he said in a voice barely above a whisper.

Might as well have been a shout, because the place was dead silent. Only noise in here were the fans circulating station air through the nearby park the Dominator kept as part of his palace.

Big guy turned back to Valentinian with a smile, standing among the carnage with a mild concussion.

"We should depart, Valentinian," he observed.

Even station security would wake up and get here soon. After that display of martial awesomeness, though, they had probably already gone back for more reinforcements.

Valentinian would have.

Nobody moved. Big guy held out a hand, like he would assist a lady into a skycar. Madame Cleray shook her head and woke from the nightmare she had apparently been expecting.

"You're right," she noted, turning to Valentinian. "I'm so glad your crew was here to help."

She turned and fled for the door before Valentinian could correct her assumption.

Did he want to? Guy had been asking for a job.

Dude cocked his head and smiled at him now, like he was offering Valentinian an out, if he wanted it.

But you know what? There were a lot of crazy folks out there with fists and guns. Valentinian and Artaxerxes had had to fast-talk their way out of trouble more than once.

Being able to punch your way to the door of an angry bar had a certain appeal of its own.

"Let's go," Valentinian decided aloud, racing to catch up with Madame Cleray.

Out the door, she had stopped suddenly. Valentinian almost ran into her again, hoping that she hadn't just spotted the Gendarmes. Although, considering the display of badassery back there, they might have just waved from a distance as they called in the Caelons, the Dominion's elite Assault Cavalry troopers.

"Where are you docked?" she said as he came alongside.

Oh, right. It had all been paperwork and electronic messages before now. She'd never been physically aboard, instead taking a three-Dee tour of the space.

"This way," Valentinian said, grabbing her arm just enough to drag her the other direction.

That nearly got him punched as she wriggled away angrily at the sudden contact. Maybe she'd go for his eyes with her claws, but he was not about to stay put to get arrested.

Instead, Valentinian dropped her hand and moved towards a nearby staff stairwell. Never get yourself trapped in an elevator when fleeing shore patrol or gendarmes. Important lesson every spacer learns eventually.

Down two long flights as fast as he could move, Valentinian had to stop at the first landing and look up. Cleray had made enough noise clacking down the metal stairs that he could track her, but the big guy moved like a jaguar.

Eerily silent in combat-looking boots that came almost to his knees.

Valentinian found his platform and palmed the switch to open the door, vibrating with impatience as the hatch retracted into the bulkhead.

Nobody on the other side as he emerged. They were on Deck Eleven now. The seedier parts of the station that the beautiful people never saw, where cargo came and went behind pretty sets designed to protect their delicate sensibilities.

Because he could, Valentinian ran. Cleray kept up, in spite of the heels. Big guy wasn't even breathing heavy.

Deck Eleven, Arm Three stuck out of the side of the station like a middle finger. All the big ships docked on Arms Two and Six to handle major cargo loads. Three was for the unfavored children. Or cheap bastards like him.

Metal floors with scratches and stains underfoot. Walls last painted maybe a decade ago. Not a single plant anywhere in sight. Industrial misery, down here where that was all the people around here needed.

Nobody emerged from a side door as they got close, smiling at him with a badge on their chest and a shock pistol in their hand. Hopefully, either he had outrun news of a bar fight or nobody was wishing to press charges right now.

Nash had started it, after all. Cameras would show that. And one of his bouncers had thrown the first punch. Just bad luck they ran into *Pain Incarnate* in blue and gray back there.

Valentinian pulled his card-reader from the inside pocket of his jacket and pressed it against the locking mechanism, pressing his thumb to the lifesign imprint. The two machines argued for a second, and then bolts retracted noisily into the bulkhead and the airlock door started to beep. A moment later, it moved outward, forcing Valentinian to the side.

Last time he had been chased like this, he had slid around the heavy door as soon as he could fit, and then triggered the override to slam it back shut again once he was in the airlock and legally aboard his own ship.

Couldn't really do that today, so he turned and watched the long walkway to make sure no uniforms were headed this directions.

Ten more seconds, and they'd be safe.

Cleray pulled her card-reader and began typing.

"Deck Eleven, Three-Three?" she asked, looking around.

"That's right," Valentinian nodded nervously. "Who are you contacting?"

"The girls," the woman looked at him with a barely suppressed eyeroll. "We have a contract, so they need to get aboard as soon as they can, before Nash finds them. And there will be a cargo sled full of gear as well."

Right. The girls. How could he forget a contract to transport a team of *nubile virgin dancers* from planet to planet for six months, along with a Dancemaster, a Songmaster, and a Chastitymaster and the others?

Dear Lord, just let me get aboard the ship. Way harder to arrest us, that way.

Big guy loomed close.

Crap, forgot him as well.

Valentinian pulled him close enough to whisper up to the giant.

"I guess you're hired," Valentinian shared a grin with the guy. "What gear do you need to grab?"

"It's in a locker up a level in the transient housing," the man replied just as quietly.

"Can you get it and get back here without being arrested?" Valentinian asked.

"Fifteen minutes," the man said.

"Comm code is Four-Seven-Six-Nine when you get back," Valentinian said. "Hey, you got a name?"

For a moment, the big man glared down at him, like he needed to remember something, and then relented.

"Dave," he said simply.

"Dave?" Valentinian was aghast. "That's it? What's it short for?"

"Nothing, just Dave."

And the guy was gone.

Dave? Valentinian had never met somebody with such a short name. Like, ever.

"Where's he going?" Cleray demanded, turning to watch Dave jog silently away.

"To get some things we left aboard station in our rush to get gone," Valentinian told her. "Let's get aboard now, and then wait for everyone else to arrive."

"Good idea," she said, striding importantly by him, into the massive aft airlock.

Valentinian keyed the systems to shut the airlock, and thought he caught a sniff of disapproval from Madame Cleray.

Like maybe a freighter like this should have been spotlessly clean and freshly painted.

Right. With the margins he normally ran?

If she was really offended, her girls could always paint the place in their spare time. Valentinian wouldn't argue. And this was just the passenger airlock. Wait until she saw what the big cargo airlock looked like.

He grinned with anticipation. She had walked the ship in three-Dee, stains and all, so it wasn't like this was new. If anything, it was cleaner than the three-Dee had been. Artaxerxes had cleaned up some before he left, what with all the nervous energy of going to meet his future spouse.

The outer door closed and the bolts set. The inner door began to beep and open onto the cargo deck of *Longshot Hypothesis*. Valentinian let himself breathe.

Safe.

Inside the big cargo bay were both cargo sleds currently docked to the side and plugged in to keep the batteries topped off. Two full decks of open space in here, since the volume was actually designed to slide in a pair of standard Anuradhan cargo pods, ten by ten by thirty meters, with clearance to walk around them on all sides and work.

The Dominion economy didn't work anything like the planet Anuradha, which had built the original vessel that became *Longshot Hypothesis*. After the Dominion had conquered and finally subdued the place a few years ago, their ships were stupidly cheap, right at the moment when Valentinian had just enough winnings and hustle to buy something, as prices collapsed and everyone else upgraded their rides.

Valentinian had made his margins since then by hauling small, priority goods point to point, and supplementing with paying passengers who either wanted to rough it, or needed to go places that the big, luxury lines didn't serve adequately.

There wasn't a box in here bigger than a two meter cube right now, although that would change when Solaria Femina got here with all their crap.

He led Cleray forward, through the inner bulkhead that separated the cargo bay from the engineering spaces. The hallway here was three meters wide, but he had all the doors closed and locked. No reason a civilian should be getting into his life support, computers, or auxiliary power reactors. They might want access to the machine shop at some point, but she could ask politely.

"Here's the elevator," Valentinian pressed the button and opened the space.

"What's through there?" she pointed forward at another bulkhead hatch, again locked, next to the stairwell to the upper deck.

"My cabin and the crew's space," Valentinian replied tartly. "We'll stay down here most of the time, except when we join you for meals."

"Okay," she decided, entering the elevator.

Valentinian joined her in the small space, staying as far away as he could while she pressed the button and they rode up a deck.

They came out in the passenger lounge, running out the port arm.

Longshot Hypothesis was built like a capital-Y, with the bridge at the fork below and the base backed up against the station for cargo. The upper deck here had a nice kitchen more-or-less above the bridge, with a lounge to port and a wardroom/dining hall to starboard. Three small cabins out each arm off a long hallway, with a small head and fresher unit at each end, and then storage and access to the oversized Anuradhan engines that hung from the ends of the spars.

Valentinian had no idea how twenty people would be crammed into a space that would crowd twelve, but again, she had presumably toured the ship and read the specs. He suspected that the nine dancers would end up in three cabins, with Madame Cleray having one to herself and everyone else crammed in wherever they would fit.

Her money was good and he could always lock hatches. The only time they would have to interact would be when the girls wanted to practice routines in the cleared-out cargo bay, and he, or Dave now, needed to do some maintenance in there.

He'd burn that bridge when they got there. Anybody who brought along a Chastitymaster wasn't going to let the girls out of her sight for a moment, so interactions would probably be limited to dinners.

And feeding him and Dave was in the contract.

Now he just needed to get the girls aboard and settled.

And figure out who the hell this guy was that he had apparently just hired.

[2]
DAVE

THE MAN who had introduced himself as *Dave* slipped into a side corridor quietly. The last thing he needed right now was to be arrested by station security, but that had been the only way to keep Madame Cleray's apparent ex-partner from causing more trouble with Dave's planned escape from Dominion Prime.

There was no way in Creation that his documentation would stand up to any sort of serious scrutiny here. Later, when they got out to the fringes of the Dominion, absolutely. Even better if Tarasicodissa's travels took him to other stellar nations.

Dave could happily disappear, never to be dragged back to the Dominion. Assuming the people who might eventually find out who he really was would ever take him alive.

There was always that.

He had memorized the back corridors of the station months ago, planning this move, so it didn't take that long to find the one he wanted. It felt odd, skulking like this, when previously he had marched right down the middle of most corridors with his pride.

Things were going to have to change, he could see that, but right now, his instincts for violence would probably serve him better.

Up a flight of harsh, metal stairs, probably painted a dingy white about the time he was born. Dave made no sound, and heard no others in this column of air.

He steeled himself to look like a casual spacer, a civilian who belonged here, if anyone happened along. He opened the door and quickly slipped out, closing it behind him and moving. The crowds in this hallway weren't all that bad, so he had some social cover as he walked.

Few of the people in sight were anywhere close to his height, but there was nothing he could do about it, except to not wear his old boots that had the extra lifts in the heel that had been designed to make him look even taller. Likewise, the old armor he had worn everywhere in public had been padded internally to make his silhouette massive.

And he wasn't wearing that damned mask.

He wondered why the Caelon troops never revolted, having to hide inside a full face helmet for their entire lives, but they were all volunteers, so he supposed they saw that armor as a badge of honor.

Good for them.

Some of the crowd he was with followed him into the transient housing block. The place was anonymous and cheap, which had been his first requirement when escaping. His estranged wife would never think to look here, nor would others, at least until all the usual ideas failed to pan out.

Hopefully, he'd be in deep space by then.

Dave pulled out his own card-reader and called up his

identity papers on the screen as he approached the wall locker where he had stashed his gear earlier.

The picture was an ugly compromise. It had to look enough different from his old life that someone randomly scanning portals like this wouldn't immediately recognize him, while at the same time looking enough like his current face to pass casual inspection.

If they got to looking at his fingerprints, he was doomed anyway.

With no way to rely on someone else to modify an old picture of himself, Dave had secretly and laboriously taught himself the necessary skills to do the work. Some of the rest he had been able to bribe or order the work done, in small enough batches that nobody should be able to assemble the whole picture until much, much later.

Or they would locate him. Whether his wife dragged him back to his old life or had him killed outright would probably hinge on her mood when they found him.

Best not to find out.

Dave listened to the locks accept the image and open themselves with a quiet thunk. Inside was a single bag, the sort of blue duffel that an off-duty Caelon might sling over a shoulder while on leave. At least that was the image he hoped to present.

He had wondered how much of his old life he could sneak along with him, but in the end decided that none of it would work. Too many clues to what he would prefer to be a shadowy past, if inspected.

He had brought along a brand new pair of blades, one for training and one with edged steel, but neither had ever seen the interior of a dojo and both were anonymous, beyond marking his class and background.

The heavy flamer pistol, on the other hand, had seen hard use over the years. Contacts had smuggled it to him back when he first decided to change his life. Serial numbers had been removed with a pocket laser at some point long ago, making it untraceable, but doing nothing to the lethality of the hunk of black metal.

Dave expected to be wearing it regularly, if some of the stories of the fringe elements of the Dominion and neighboring nations were to be believed. At least he knew how to use the thing, most likely better than any of the people he encountered out there.

For the rest, a couple changes of clothes that would get him somewhere else, and enough credits on hand and in secret accounts that he could buy more specific things as he needed them.

At the last minute, he had broken his vow and kept one thing from his past. One thing that could possibly identify him, if someone really knew the man who had become Dave Hall. A book, given to him originally by his father. Of course, if they were that close to capturing him, all it would do was confirm the truth, to the six people who knew the story.

That was a risk he was willing to take.

Dave closed the locker and turned to study the space around him. Nobody seemed to be paying him any attention, and that was all he could hope for right now. There was no reason for anyone to be alert, unless they were already secretly informers for the White Hats, and in that case, he needed to outrun the memory of Dave Hall making its slow, laborious way through the Dominion bureaucracy.

Those people would eventually put it all together, he assumed. But Dave Hall hadn't rented this bed and this locker, either. False trails and multiple identities were all that would get him aboard *Longshot Hypothesis*. From there, it was his native cunning, something that had served him well for fifty years.

Dave smiled to himself as he emerged back into the hallway. Around a corner, he pulled out his card-reader and stepped back into the service hallway he had used before.

Empty. Good.

Quickly, he pulled a small screwdriver from his bag and opened the back of the card-reader. As he put the screwdriver back, the door opened suddenly.

A woman emerged, apparently looking backwards over her shoulder. She plowed right into Dave and knocked the card-reader, chip, and back plate from his hands.

"Oh my God, I'm so sorry," she stopped, hands to her mouth. "I didn't see you there."

Dave suppressed a growl.

"It's fine," he muttered, looking around for all the pieces.

"Here," she said, dropping to her knees. "Let me help."

Dave took a deep breath and remained silent. The faster she was gone, the better.

He knelt, trying not to smell her perfume, or notice the fact that she had turned away from him and all he could see of her right now was brown hair and a bottom outlined in pants a size too small. She was young, maybe five years older than his daughter at most.

Six months of celibacy didn't help his state of mind. He moved around her quickly as she grabbed the card-reader and sat up into a kneeling position.

"Oh, crap, I broke it," she held it out like a scared kitten.

Dave glanced at the open and empty back and then raced after the identity chip and the back plate, grabbing those before she got more involved.

"I can fix it," he said quickly, taking it from her hand.

"I feel like I owe you," she said, her voice changing, growing deeper and slower.

Seriously? Are you flirting with me, young lady? Do you have any idea who I am?

But of course she didn't. She'd be screaming in fear or running for the authorities if she did.

"It's fine," he repeated, starting to stand so he could extricate himself from this encounter.

"No, seriously," she pressed her case, resting a hand on his forearm as she rose with him. "Let me buy you dinner as an apology."

Dave cut off all lines of thought and smiled grimly at her.

"Unfortunately, I'm late for departure already, and the captain's holding the ship for me to get back to the ship," Dave more or less told the truth. "Perhaps next time I'm on the station?"

It sounded like a good way to deflect her. There was no chance in hell Dave Hall was ever voluntarily stepping foot on Dominion Prime, so it was even a promise he could make without lying.

Voluntarily being the key. And she probably would lose interest in him, if he was being drug across the deck in chains.

"I'll chirp you my contact information," she said, pulling out her card-reader from an inside pocket of the light jacket she was wearing.

Dave hadn't been paying that much attention to the rest of her, once he got distracted by her bottom.

Short woman that somehow still conveyed willowy strength. Brown hair in a pageboy cut that framed green eyes. Well-dressed in red pants and a gold top, with a black jacket over that. Stylish, and he had spent too much time around people for whom style was the only avenue of competition left to them.

Quickly, Dave palmed his old chip and slipped Dave Hall into the card-reader. Easier than arguing with her at this point and making the sort of scene where she might remember him all the more vividly.

The card-reader came alive as he clipped the back more or less in place, and Dave Hall suddenly existed somewhere besides his own imagination.

"I'm Amalathea," she said, a touch breathily for his benefit as both machines chirped happily. "Amalathea Parsakoutenos. Looking forward to hearing from you."

She left things dangling, but Dave wasn't ready to chirp her back his information. No reason to get her executed by the White Hats, just for being friendly, helpful, and flirtatious.

"Dave Hall," he replied, turning and attacking the staircase like an orbital drop with a ticking bomb somewhere behind him.

Now was really not the time to make new friends.

[3]
VALENTINIAN

Something was wrong.

Valentinian had managed to escape trouble and jail as many times as he had over the last few years by listening to that little voice in his head that smelled danger. Most of the time it hadn't led him astray, not counting bar fights, which were frequently random things he happened into, rather than starting.

The flavor of life out on the concourse had changed. No other way to describe it. And it wasn't just that he had gone into the Armory on the main deck and grabbed himself a shock pistol and a holster. That was kinda standard, since most of the places *Longshot Hypothesis* docked or landed weren't as polite and well-run as Dominion Prime. And he could do that as long as he was standing on his own deck and didn't enter the station again.

There weren't more gendarmes than normal moving around out there. Well, maybe a few more, but nothing out of the ordinary.

They were moving with more deliberation. That was it. More focus. Like they were looking for someone or something, but didn't want to broadcast it over the speakers and alert the victim that the net was closing in on them.

Valentinian was still twitchy. The cargo airlock was open, and a team of station stevedores was about halfway through loading the several pallets of junk and stuff Madame Cleray had brought into the cargo bay.

Nash hadn't made an appearance, but Valentinian was technically standing on his own deck, on this side of the airlock line. He couldn't fire at Nash or one of his people if they stayed on the station part of the concourse, but they couldn't do anything to him, either.

Not without someone coming onto his deck uninvited and being charged with piracy. Good way to walk out an open airlock into space, doing that. Especially on Dominion Prime. Doubly so when the gendarmes were acting twitchy.

Madame Cleray was standing immediately beside him, checking things off with a clipboard and a shrill, demanding voice. Valentinian figured that anyone trying to get past her would get a faceful of hurt in the bargain. She was even more nervous than he was.

Who the hell was Nash and what kind of power did the man wield, anyway? No easy way to ask that right now. Maybe once they got detached from the station.

Valentinian had gotten introduced to everyone once, but didn't bother with names right now. The nine dancers were almost impossible to tell apart, anyway, as each of them almost looked like younger clones of Madame Cleray with hair in different cuts and colors.

While that might lead to some interesting fantasies later, right now it was just plain spooky. Even worse than everything else going on.

Only the Dancemaster was speaking at this point. She looked like a former close-combat instructor Cleray had maybe recruited away from the Caelons. Short graying hair, wiry muscles, hawk-like visage, angry voice.

Valentinian had always thought that any woman could be attractive, if she wanted to be, regardless of the arrangement of her face. Meeting Kostantina Tarchaneiotes, the Dancemaster, just might disabuse him of that notion. That woman seemed angry at the entire galaxy, and willing to do something about it.

But between the two women watching the dock like hungry predators, nobody was going to be sneaking aboard. Just in case, Valentinian had locked everything anyway. Nobody but him could get into the rest of the ship right now.

Well, he supposed someone with enough energy might somehow try to hack the systems into the forward airlock, the one just off the bridge, but he had added manual alarms there, too. Those had become necessary, after the last time that had happened.

So he felt safe on his deck. Dave Hall couldn't do any more than Cleray or her girls, at least until Valentinian programmed them all into the system. He could explain that as having redone security while Hall was gone.

That wouldn't make the newest employee stand out. He hoped.

Speak of the devil.

It was eerie watching the man move. Valentinian had never seen someone so big move with such fluid grace. Made him jealous, but the girls frequently went for the bad-boy space captain, so that wouldn't be a problem, next station they landed at.

But one minute it was just stevedores, and the next Hall was standing right in front of him with a serious-looking smile on his face and a bag slung over his shoulder.

Valentinian decided to play it casual.

"About time," he announced, treating the man like an old-time employee. "You take over here and make sure nobody causes any trouble. I'll start the pre-flight."

The wry smile on Hall's face said a lot, but the man slipped the big bag from his shoulder and slid it off to one side.

Madame Cleray seemed much happier to have the big man handy, but Valentinian wasn't offended. He felt the same way.

Valentinian had just keyed the new code to unlock the hatch between the cargo bay and engineering when Hall's voice echoed around him like an apocalypse or something.

"Captain?" Hall yelled, almost formally.

Valentinian turned around to see a whole new crop of trouble standing just outside his ship. All the girls of Solaria Femina and their minders had huddled off to one side of the bay like frightened sheep, and the Dancemaster and Hall appeared to be blocking everything else.

Valentinian looked past them and swallowed the profanity before it escaped his mouth.

Trouble. Not just trouble. *Serious trouble.*

He had been expecting gendarmes to show up and question him. That was fine, since they were habitually unarmed, civilian soldiers. Bureaucrats, more than anything. And there were two gendarmes with this group.

The other five were White Hats. The Dominion's internal security force. Burgundy bodysuits, while the gendarmes wore blue, with the bonus white berets that had the gold Dominion logo over the left ear.

And guns. Four had pulse carbines slung at their hips. The officer just had a pistol.

As if that made her any less dangerous.

He took a deep breath quietly and ambled back over to the volcano of ugly that threatened to erupt and spray mud and pain all over his cargo bay. Who the hell was Nash, that he could sick White Hats on them, and do it that quickly?

"Valentinian Tarasicodissa?" the woman asked as he got close. "Captain of *Longshot Hypothesis?*"

If you scaled Dave Hall down to someone average height for a woman, but kept the hard muscles and sure movement, and made her a woman, she'd be standing right in front of him. The pistol on her hip was a badge of authority, as was the burgundy jumpsuit that looked painted on. He focused on her eyes, rather than admiring her figure or her pretty face.

Thoughts of black widows kept racing across his mind.

"That's right," Valentinian replied breezily. "What seems to be the problem?"

This was already way past the point of paying a fine and getting a good talking to from a stationmaster. White Hats didn't play around.

"No immediate problem," she even smiled grimly at him. "We're inspecting every vessel before it leaves port for stowaways."

Valentinian cocked his head at her, and then shrugged. Huh?

"Any problems if we board your vessel, Captain?" she asked.

It even sounded polite.

If you didn't know any better.

"None," Valentinian said, fresh out of ideas.

Fortunately he wasn't smuggling anything on this trip, either.

"Is there anybody aboard?" the woman stepped over the line in the deck and got close enough that he could smell the breath mint she had apparently eaten at some point this morning. She might have even smiled at him.

Rather than just step back, Valentinian also turned

slightly, pivoting on his foot and keeping elbows in. Physical contact, even accidentally, probably got him thrown in a brig somewhere.

"Just myself and my First Mate," Valentinian said, pointing to Dave. "My new passengers were in the process of loading equipment and supplies, but all of them are in immediate sight."

The White Hat woman turned and stared up at Dave like she had just realized he was a human, and not a tree. The man was huge.

"Papers?" she demanded politely.

Valentinian watched Dave turn sideways carefully, so everyone could see him pull the card-reader out of his back pocket, rather than a knife or a gun. A man who had done this before. Dave keyed the front and typed in a quick code before handing it to the woman delicately.

"Hall?" she studied him for a moment.

"Yes, ma'am," Dave replied.

"You remain here with the gendarmes," she ordered, turning back to Valentinian with an unreadable smile. "You will accompany myself and my team."

Well, so much for even the remote chance of leaving on time. Valentinian turned and took a step, glancing back to make sure the woman followed. Her four friends weren't far behind that.

Man, somebody must be pissed.

But old Nash was in for a surprise if he went looking for trouble right now.

Through the first hatch, into the engineering spaces. The armory and workout room got inspected. Water storage tanks were physically opened from the top by one of the women with the officer. The machine shop next. Life support, which was Dominion standard instead of what the ship had been built with. Anuradhan tech had been at least a generation behind.

Valentinian hadn't done the refurb that pulled out the hydroponics room and turned it into an armory, but he approved. He'd have just killed all the fish and plants anyway. And all of his weapons were legally registered somewhere, just not here.

The Overdrive generator was Dominion standard as well, replacing the older model when engineering got overhauled. All three Auxiliary Power Reactors were original equipment, as were the computer systems that handled the nav system, entertainment, and the full systems cores.

Forward, she followed him into the Primary quarters, down the two quick steps from the Engineering deck. The cockpit was in the center, with his cabin on the port side and what would become Dave's to starboard, plus the head, a galley/rec room, and the forward airlock mostly used on planetary surfaces.

"Just two of you?" the woman demanded.

"That's right," he replied with the slightest bit of irk to his voice. "Passengers are largely self-contained upstairs."

And so he had to show everyone the upper deck. He and the woman rode the elevator while the others climbed the stairs, presumably so some stowaway couldn't double back on them.

Or something. Whatever floats your boat, paranoid lady.

The main kitchen was centerline, just over the bridge and aft a little. The laundry room and passenger consumables storage behind that were both empty and almost immaculate, but that would change tomorrow, assuming he had a small tribe of people living up here in a space comfortable for six.

The lounge was to port, with three cabins, a head, and access to the port engine. Starboard was identical, save for the lounge being a dining hall.

Valentinian leaned back against a bulkhead and waited as everybody sniffed everything.

The woman officer walked right up into his personal space and looked up at him.

If Valentinian stood up right now, he would brush against her chest, so he kept his hands behind him and kept his weight back.

"Everything appears to be in order, Captain," she announced from close enough to breathe on him.

What the hell is your issue, lady?

But he didn't say that. Didn't even think it too loudly. Just smiled vaguely at her.

"I try to run a tight ship," he replied.

She smiled. Maybe a smile. Maybe painful gas bubbling up from the depths of hell.

You never knew with White Hats.

"Tight can be good, Tarasicodissa," she said in a warmer tone.

Are you kidding me? I'd rather take monastic vows than touch you, princess.

She wasn't ugly. Was actually rather pleasant looking. Hard body from working out. Nice, regular features. Pretty, blue eyes.

But she wore a White Hat. The Dominion's police sledgehammer. Even the Caelons feared those people.

And she smiled expectantly at him.

Suddenly, Valentinian was fourteen again and taking a girl on a blind date, the kind that parents had arranged, to a social dance. The kind of girl his mother describe as *having a great personality*. You know the type.

He played it cool then, and cooler now, just arching an eyebrow at the officer as if to ask a multitude of questions.

Apparently, she was satisfied. At least as satisfied as those people can be without pulling wings off of flies for fun.

She stepped back out of his space with a prim, knowing smile and gathered up her team.

"We'll talk again," she promised in a voice that nearly convinced Valentinian to leave Dominion space forever and see what kinds of trade he might find out in Wildspace beyond Laurentia. It was that or maybe head all the way to Asherah.

Anything that didn't involve a personal inspection by this woman.

Because he knew how that would turn out.

Valentinian let her lead and lagged well behind them going down the stairs, partly to make sure nobody left anything or anybody behind. Not much he could do about any bugs or trackers somebody had stashed in one of the chambers when he wasn't looking, but that wasn't going to stop him from looking for them.

After they left station.

Downstairs and aft, Valentinian joined Dave and watched as Madame Cleray and her entire team got personally inspected, along with a random assortment of their boxes. No, strike that, the bigger boxes only. None of the small ones.

What the hell was going on?

Valentinian glanced at Dave in that universal language of gender that transcends language, but the big guy just shrugged back at him.

Finally, the woman cop seemed mollified. She and her people walked back across the line until they were legally on the station again, and not on *Longshot Hypothesis*. The woman in the white beret smiled at him and departed. Madame Cleray and her troupe got everything inside the ship as fast as they could move, and Valentinian closed up the airlock.

They could sort it all out from warp. He wanted gone.

"Now what?" Madame Cleray appeared in his face, but she was a pale imitation of trouble at this point, and after a moment, she realized it, relaxing and taking a half step back at the sudden, thunderous scowl on Valentinian's face.

He nodded to Dave and drew the man into his wake as he moved forward and crossed the hatch into the primary spaces. He still needed to code Dave into the system, and the best way to do that was from the bridge.

"Get your girls into their cabins," Valentinian decided. "We're leaving."

[4]
VALENTINIAN

"Any idea what the hell that was all about?" Valentinian heard his new First Mate ask as they got into the ship's cockpit.

Technically, the deck plans called it a bridge, but it was two seats, side by side with a small console between them for the overdrive systems, and matching flight controls. The view out the front window was constrained by the two arms extending overhead, but *Longshot Hypothesis* wasn't a combat gunship. Wasn't even armed.

He could fly it fine from here, and would back up to most stations with using exterior ameras anyway. The only times he generally needed the viewports in front of him involved landing on a planet.

"None," Valentinian answered after a second spent typing a password into the system between the two seats. "You sit here and type a password in."

Valentinian took the port seat and let Dave climb into the starboard one, after the big guy rocked the seat back three clicks to make leg room for himself. Artaxerxes had been shorter than Valentinian.

"So White Hats don't normally board your ship and personally inspect it?" Dave continued.

"That's the first time anybody has wanted to go beyond eyeballing the cargo bay since I've owned it," Valentinian said. "I thought maybe Nash had the jets to cause us trouble, but apparently that was unrelated."

"So now what?" Dave turned to look at him.

"So now you're employed," Valentinian said. "I'll send you a copy of the contract I had with Artaxerxes and we'll go from there. If you don't like it or don't fit in, we're going to Aestrolathia and you can depart there where I'll pay you for time served. Otherwise, we're leaving here as soon as I can get clearance from the station, and hitting warp as soon as I clear the buoys so that we won't get fined later."

"We coming back to Dominion Prime or even Cronus Prime anytime soon?" Dave seemed nervous on that thought.

The station was bad news. Valentinian could only imagine the capital world below them. The one that had spawned Dominion culture and loosed it on an unsuspecting galaxy five or six centuries ago.

"Between you and me, that White Hat babe has almost convinced me to leave Dominion space forever," Valentinian admitted. "Maybe even spend the rest of my life out in Wildspace. Know what I mean?"

"Oh, yeah, I'm with you there," Dave said. "Wouldn't hurt my feelings, either."

"Which reminds me," Valentinian said. "We need to talk about your past soon, so line up whatever lies you plan to spin and make them sound good, okay? Until then, I'm getting us away from the scene of whatever crime happened while I still can."

He liked the way Dave's face went still at those words. Like he had maybe been expecting Valentinian to be a simple innocent who would accept any story, hook, line, AND sinker.

Valentinian smiled up at the big man and turned his attention to the communications board.

"Dominion Prime Flight Control, this is *Longshot Hypothesis*," he said as the radio came live. "Docked in Eleven-Three-Three. Requesting departure window and lane assignment."

"Stand by, Eleven-Three-Three," a lazy-sounding man replied a second later.

Valentinian sucked air all the way to his toes and tried to pretend that it was just another day at the office. Bar fights, White Hats, stowaways, and virgins were normal things in the life of a tramp captain, right?

Valentinian had expected Hall to stir uncomfortably as the time stretched, but the big, warrior monk just sat perfectly still, like a statue someone had snuck into the cockpit when nobody was looking.

"Eleven-Three-Three, this is Flight Control," a different voice, a sultry, female voice came back. "You are clear to unlock and depart. Lane assignment and flight path from terminal area have been transmitted. Safe journeys."

Safe journeys? What the hell was going on? Nobody ever said something like that.

Then he recognized the second voice.

Death ran a chilly hand across his neck and down his back.

"Was that…?" Dave hesitated.

"Yeah," Valentinian nodded.

The woman in the white beret.

Left his deck and went right down to flight control, maybe so she could say goodbye? Or know what planet he was visiting next?

Valentinian keyed the internal speakers.

"All hands, brace for departure," he said, pressing the lock controls. "Now."

Aft, the bolts holding the ship to the station retracted with a hollow thump that echoed through the skin of the ship. Compressed air jets separated the ship from the station, and Valentinian brought the big engines forward live enough to provide a purring stroll into the darkness.

Much as he wanted to slam them to the stops, the fines weren't worth the satisfaction. Not today, at least.

Paranoia made him activate a rear camera on one of his screens and then toggle to the view in both airlocks, on the off-chance that that White Hat had decided to stow herself away and follow him.

Valentinian knew girls dug his look. He worked hard at casually dressing and appearing just rugged enough to trigger the right hormones in the women he dealt with. Black pants with a green stripe down the outer seam. Collarless egg-cream shirt in a soft linen, covered over with a light, black jacket with the same green at certain seams.

Dangerous, but approachable. Bad boy, but not all *that* bad. Redeemable, if you wanted to *work* at it, honey.

But, oh shit did he not want a White Hat responding to those cues. Gods only knew what she might do. Or where she might stalk him.

But there was nothing back there. Just a growing gap separating *Longshot Hypothesis* from the station. Him from her. And Nash. And whatever other trouble was brewing back there.

Quickly, Valentinian programmed the lane into the system and turned on the autopilot. It would take them half an hour just to get to the first buoy. Another ten minutes or so after that and he could light the overdrive system, spin up a warp bubble, and shift to FTL.

He turned his attention back to Dave and studied the

man. Bad-ass, warrior monk. Probably has a sword in that bag. Crazed berserkers that hadn't conquered the entire galaxy already because they spent as much time fussing with each other as they did on their campaigns.

"I'm going to skip the first few questions I would have normally asked you," Valentinian said, making sure that the hatch to the cockpit was closed before he spoke. "That way, I can be just a fool later, and not a willing accomplice. Good enough?"

"Good enough," Dave turned towards him. "I had it all. Power. Glory. Success. Lived a really good life for a very long time. Woke up on the wrong side of the bed one morning."

"When was this?" Valentinian asked, setting timelines in his head.

"About a year ago," Dave said. "I wanted out, but that wasn't a job you could just chuck out the airlock and walk away from. Plus I thought it was just a phase."

"Mid-life crisis?" Valentinian nodded.

"Turned out to be one, in retrospect, yeah," Dave agreed. "Plus I have a wife, however estranged the woman is. Was. Two kids, about your age or a little older. And friends, allies, and enemies. So getting out took a lot of planning and other things."

"Did you have to kill someone?" Valentinian asked automatically.

Dave grimaced and waggled his head back and forth.

"You know what?" Valentinian raced ahead before the big man could say anything. "Don't answer that. I don't want to know the truth, do I?"

"Fool or willing accomplice. Your words," Dave said with a grim voice.

"Fool it is," Valentinian said harshly. "Plausible deniability later. I posted a job opening. You answered. I needed your particular skill set more than any of the other applicants, and hired you."

"Anybody else even apply yet?" Dave asked.

"No, but that's beside the point," Valentinian grinned. "Most of the people I would have hired would have gotten all our asses kicked in that bar. So thank you for saving my ass. Our asses. We're going to make a nice margin on this contract, assuming Madame Cleray plays us even remotely straight."

"You have your doubts?" Dave asked, turning serious.

"Woman like that is always surfing to the main chance," Valentinian replied. "Saw that in her eyes. She'd burn us in a heartbeat, if she felt she needed to. But I knew that, going in. And she's a little afraid of you, so we've got that going for us."

"And the rest?" Dave pressed.

"Pretty, kewpie dolls, as far as I'm concerned," Valentinian said. "Wouldn't fuck any of them with your dick. The Nutritionist, I think her name was Hiranur, is the only one that seemed even remotely human, compared to the hostile predators the rest of them present as. She's too old for me to really take serious, but my dad always said the older woman was a better choice, because she knew what she wanted, what she was doing, and didn't have nearly the silly notions of the young ones. And they'll cook you breakfast in the morning. And she has to be a good cook, if Cleray hired her for this gig."

Dave laughed with him. It was a bonding thing between guys, but they were all kind of stuck in this situation right now. The only other male on the ship right now was the Songmaster, Fahrettin something-or-other, who had introduced himself as *ambivalently, aggressively multi-sexual.*

Whatever the hell that meant.

"So now what?" Dave asked as they fell into a sudden silence.

"I got troubles," Valentinian replied. "You got troubles. Cleray and her girls got troubles. I'm trying to outrun them to Aestrolathia and see what we can do to wriggle off that hook before the big, hungry fish comes nosing around."

"So how can I help?" Dave asked simply.

It was clear he wanted to say more, but Valentinian had drawn a bright line on purpose.

Don't tell me things that will get me executed later, unless and until I need to know, okay?

"Your cabin is out the door and on the starboard side," Valentinian said. "Go stow your gear and get settled. We'll be clear to spin up a warp bubble in a while, assuming nobody comes after us with sirens wailing. Once we're in warp, I'll walk you through the basic maintenance tasks that you'll handle, once we get the girls all squared away upstairs."

"Got it," Dave said, rising.

"One other thing," Valentinian interrupted his departure. "Normally, passengers stay upstairs at all times, but they will need the cargo bay to practice, so we'll have the girls underfoot a lot. Keep them out of engineering spaces unless you clear it with me first, and keep them out of the primary space forward at all times. That means nobody in your bunk, even for a quickie. It can wait until we get planetside at Aestrolathia."

"Trust me, it will be longer than that," Dave promised in a hard voice. "Nobody I've seen here will turn my head."

"Good," Valentinian shooed him out of the cockpit.

He felt the same way. Even the nutritionist was only a possibility, unless she approached him and *demanded* a roll in the hay.

Valentinian kept flashing back to the woman in the white beret. Somehow, he knew he'd be seeing her again.

[5]
KYRIAKI

Inspector Kyriaki Apokapes watched as the ship detached from the station and engaged engines, drawing away as if it would disappear into the darkness.

The thought distressed her. Which, in turn, pissed her the fuck off.

Kyriaki was not a woman whose head was turned by just any man. Especially not a rogue like Tarasicodissa, regardless of how dashing he might think he was.

She wondered what she might have found had her inspection of *Longshot Hypothesis* been in greater detail. What secrets the man might be hiding.

Orders had been merely to closely inspect every ship and container leaving, checking for stowaways attempting to flee the station. Nobody had any clue why Operations was running at such a high and terse tempo, but everyone in a position of authority was harsh and sharp this morning.

Kyriaki turned to the flight control officer with a sharp glare.

"You've confirmed this flight plan?" she demanded.

An officer wearing a white beret was not someone to be

challenged, unless you had powerful backers, or maybe were bored with this career and wanted something harder and farther away from the centers of power. Like a prison farm on a desert planet.

"This is what he filed for departure," the man corrected her. "Once he clears terminal control, what course he plots is unknown and unknowable, Inspector."

"Very good," she decided.

The White Hats were everywhere. Valentinian Tarasicodissa couldn't run far enough to escape her once she figured out what it was that drew her to the man. Even the borders of the Dominion were just a suggestion at the limitations of her power if he got her angry enough. The place where she might have to change into mufti and continue her journey as a supposed civilian if she found it necessary to bring him to justice the hard way.

He was hiding something, but she couldn't tell what. And it wasn't enough to do more than just file her reports and wait for orders.

She turned and departed the flight control room, gathering up her team from a lounge outside and returning to barracks. The rest disappeared quickly, resting or eating until the next orders or the next vessel needing to be boarded.

Kyriaki returned to her office. It was small and sterile. The White Hats did not do personality. All was given in service of the Dominion, with no time or effort given for individuality.

Not if you wanted to get ahead.

She was not a member of the Solar Party. Was not allowed to even consider joining them at some future point if she wanted to keep this job. The Party controlled the government, and all power therein except the White Hats.

Her organization was outside Party control, to keep the Party itself in line.

Who watches the watchers?

We do.

The Party was a check on the Dominator and the Dominion military. The White Hats were a check on the Party. Sheer size kept the White Hats from dominating, as they were a tiny, elite force envisioned as a scalpel, cutting away at treasonous growths with surgical precision, as an alternative to dropping the Dominion Armada or a Caelon Assault Cavalry brigade on a problem.

Midafternoon, she was summoned to the main office on Prime Deck.

Alone.

A briefing for only officers: Inspectors and Inquisitors. Maybe an explanation for why everyone was so tense.

The room where they gathered was small. They numbered less than twenty, even on the station that was the seat of Dominion power.

Kyriaki took her seat as the Ambassador strode to a lectern at the front of the classroom.

While everyone of them wore the burgundy bodysuit that was as much a mark of their power and organization as their white beret, the Ambassador wore loose robes over his, almost a toga in the way it draped. She supposed that it made him look less threatening, to anyone foolish enough to believe a man like Rodosthenis Mataraci wasn't far more dangerous that she was.

He might only be in his late fifties, tall and gaunt and bald, but his face had lines that suggested they had been put there by pain and a chisel, rather than aging. Eyes filled with hazel fire gazed out at them.

The Ambassador pressed a button in front of him, and the doors locked audibly. Imposingly.

"The Dominator has been assassinated," he announced, waiting calmly for the shouts of rage and surprise to die down before he continued.

It took several seconds, even as disciplined as this force was. This Dominator had been a respected leader, even for as long as he had held power. Kyriaki had privately expected him to last perhaps as long as another decade before he took his life in ritual combat when a successor challenged.

There were no ex-Dominators. It was a job until death. Certainly, enough men and women had to die, each time one succeeded in vying for the throne.

"We have not been informed by the Household how it happened, or even when," the Ambassador finally continued. "So I cannot begin to suggest clues as to the perpetrator. Our task is simply to investigate, with what little we know, while the Armada prepares to announce the next Tournament of Domination."

The Tournament.

Kyriaki was too young to remember the previous time a Dominator took power. This one had ruled for twenty-five years, since just after she was born.

Any man or woman could enter their name in the lists, but only sixty-four were chosen by an unknown lottery to participate. Tests of Intellect washed out half, leaving thirty-two to attempt the Test of Stamina, and then sixteen for the Test of Strategy.

Eight would emerge from that challenge successful, and would be placed into mortal combat. Seven would die, and the last would become the new Dominator. There was no second place, and the person in ninth was not considered a viable threat, unless they chose to become one.

More than once over the centuries, men and women making it that far had intentionally failed at that point, thinking to challenge the eventual winner later. The White

Hats held responsibility for watching those people more than the rest.

No threat to the Dominion was allowed.

Ever.

The Ambassador did not answer questions. Nobody knew what to ask at this point, other than to pay closer attention to the world and spy things out of alignment.

Something must have shown on her face as the Ambassador dismissed them.

"Inspector Apokapes," he called as everyone rose. "A moment?"

It sounded like a request. She was not fooled.

Kyriaki moved to the end of the row and approached the front of the room carefully. Quickly, they were alone.

"Something troubles you?" he asked in a penetrating voice. "Have you a lead we might pursue?"

"I am not sure, Ambassador," she replied carefully. "Following orders this morning, we inspected and boarded several vessels departing the station. At the time, we were told only to look for contraband and stowaways, but not fleeing assassins."

"Did you see something, Kyriaki?" his eyes got intense.

"No," she said firmly. "It was more of a personal response. An emotional reaction that I cannot explain, other than to say it suggested wrongness at some deep, almost intuitive level. A vessel was loading for departure in a great hurry. The crew and a passenger had previously been involved in what station gendarmes suggest was a minor fracas in a bar on the elite level, but injuries were minimal and nobody demanded charges. Their papers were in order, but the group was large and loading was a messy event. We could have perhaps checked their papers more carefully, but my paranoia at the time was merely functional, rather than vindictive. The ship itself was clean."

He smiled at her distinction. All officers were to embody paranoia as part of their training and work. But there were times when it became necessary to *transcend*.

A thought struck her.

"Do we even know what the Dominator looks like?" she asked carefully, aware that the man only ever appeared in public wearing his black armor and fear-inducing helmet, with a voice electronically modulated and projected at all times.

"No one does," the Ambassador allowed. "As with the Caelons, who only ever appear in their battle armor. None other than members of the immediate Household. Normally, that makes it safer for the man, since no assassin would know him on sight. We have failed in ways I cannot even begin to calculate. But this ship. Tell me about it."

"*Longshot Hypothesis*," she replied. "A modified Anuradhan cargo transport. Captained by a young man named Valentinian Tarasicodissa. The charter was to transport one Lianearia Cleray and a musical troupe known as Solaria Femina to Aestrolathia."

"I have heard of them," the Ambassador nodded. "My daughter listened to their music when she was a teenager. They are still around?"

"My understanding from the paperwork and my subsequent research is that the group ages members out with ruthless regularity," Kyriaki said. "Cleray was one of the original members, twenty years ago, and continues to manage them. She had a large entourage, almost militantly organized."

"And you suspect them?" he asked.

Kyriaki shrugged.

"I question my own shadow right now," she admitted. "Nothing else I have seen in the last two days rose to the level of cognizance. Even this barely does, but something has left me feeling off about the entire venture and I cannot describe it adequately."

She dared not admit even to herself the strange, emotional reaction she had from standing too close to Tarasicodissa.

It challenged her objectivity. Threatened her competence. Pissed her off at a visceral level.

And there was more to it than merely attraction to the man.

What, she could not say. But lacking the terms to describe it did not lessen the feeling of wrongness on iota.

"Acknowledged, Inspector," the older man said. "I will review your files and station notes and see if something jumps out at me with the benefit of hindsight. Dismissed."

"Thank you, sir," she said, quickly departing and returning to her quarters.

Valentinian Tarasicodissa didn't strike her as an assassin, but something was off.

Maybe, if she was lucky, she'd get a chance to dig into his past and find his flaw.

She looked forward to talking to him again.

Perhaps even in a friendly way.

[6]
LIANEARIA

LIANEARIA HAD NOT EXPECTED the cargo bay of this new transport to have even remotely acceptable acoustics for practice, so she was pleasantly surprised, the first time the Songmaster filled it with music. The reverb was only slightly off from that of a medium-sized stage.

A simple, cotton blanket hung from the overhead catwalk, and the sound was perfect.

Lianearia watched now from that elevated perch as the music commenced and the team began to move.

She had written her first song for the group eleven years ago, after being cast out into nothingness by the previous management for the sin of turning twenty-three. Years of starvation and transience, as she tried to make a life for herself, all washed up at an age when many were only emerging from schooling.

It has been hard. But it had toughened her. Even more than the singing and dancing as an original member of the group.

For the last five years, she had written almost all of the music they performed, with the exception of the two greatest hits from the early era, which were still their signature. It was just one more way she controlled the money, paying herself royalties that frequently went right back into cash flow.

She supposed the residuals might be enough for a comfortable lifestyle, on some boring retirement world, but she was thirty-nine years old, and nowhere close to letting *them* win.

"No," she yelled. "Stop. Eslem, you're off tempo with everyone else."

The music died instantly. Lianearia fixed the Dancemaster with an angry glare. Kostantina might choreograph things well, but she had been shaped by the Dominion's Solar Guard. Military efficiency. That was good, but it did not sell the allure of virgin sexuality they needed to be successful.

"Again," Lianearia demanded. "From the very top. Eslem, step out on the second beat, rather than waiting for the first note. Otherwise, you are out of position when the group pivots."

Lianearia gestured to the Songmaster, watched Fahrettin reset the song to the top as the girls maneuvered back to the triple trio, each group facing inward while the intro built.

They had more than a week to learn the moves to two new songs. And no distractions at all, save the two men of the crew transporting them to Aestrolathia.

She had been concerned to travel with strangers but the chandler who found her *Longshot Hypothesis* had made it clear that she should specifically hire this ship. Favors owed, she supposed, but she had been unable to glean any part of a connection between the chandler and Valentinian Tarasicodissa.

It could have been worse, when she considered an extended engagement with him, or the other one. Happily, they appeared to have no interest in seducing any of

Lianearia's girls, going so far as to ignore all of them, except for the usual eyes staring at toned legs and tight bodices.

Briefly, as the music started, she had feared the need to sick Fahrettin on the two spacers, but neither seemed interested in what her Dancemaster had to offer, either. In fact, the only person either of them had showed any interest in at all was the cook, Hiranur.

Bizarre. Spacers were supposed to act like drunkards filled with braggadocio. At least all the ones she had ever encountered.

Was that why her contacts had put her in touch with this man? To show her, via *Longshot Hypothesis*, that there could be professionals out there beyond her immediate troupe?

Axarnashalic Bogomelous, *Nash*, had left a sour taste in her mouth. And charged her too much money for every single thing. Valentinian had happily accepted a flat-fee deal, when that was so rare in her industry.

At this rate, her normal margins, always razor-thin, might actually grow enough to make her happy.

Happier, anyway.

"Yes, better," she yelled as the group passed the previous point and Eslem stayed on cue.

And the ship wasn't a hunk of garbage, flying between stars with frequent breakdowns and expensive repair delays that cut into her funds.

Give her a year like this, and she might consider retiring. Or at least selling the group to someone else and letting them handle the messiness for a while.

She wasn't ruthless. That suggested a complete lack of remorse. Lianearia had much to regret. Things she had done to get by. Favors offered. Mistakes made.

At the least the girls would not be thrown to the wolves when they left. That much she could offer. Each had an investment account opened on day one, with a portion of their pay deposited into it immediately, and untouchable while they remained with the group. Not even Lianearia could access the money, except to instruct the broker to make changes rebalancing funds on an annual basis.

No girl would walk out of here broke. Or lost.

She caught movement out of the corner of her eye and saw the two men climbing the staircase on her right. Dave held a large toolbox easily in one hand as he walked.

Neither man more than glanced at the girls dancing below. And after only a week in space.

It was good. The Chastitymaster, Sümeyye, had been especially vigilant, going so far as to station herself at the top of the stairs at night to keep the girls from sneaking downstairs. What they did on their own, in their own cabins, was not her concern, as long as no men were involved.

Valentinian approached. He started to say something over the noise of the song, and thought better of it. Instead, he gestured politely for her to move to her right.

She did, splitting her attention between the careful movements below as the song built to its climax, and the two men approaching. Dave placed the box and Valentinian pulled out tool of some sort, quickly backing bolts out of the wall behind where she had been standing at the apex of the catwalk.

A panel was removed, exposing pipes and such inside.

The two men weren't talking with voice so much as with hands. It seemed Valentinian was teaching Dave how to fix something.

Was the man merely muscle? That was acceptable. She didn't think Nash would take no for an answer. At least not immediately. Eventually, he would run out of goons he could hire, or do something so outrageous in his blind anger that she could press charges.

Hopefully on a world where he didn't own any prosecutors.

The song ended.

"Good," she called, turning her attention back to the deck below. "Now, again. And focus on your hands. I want them moving like a school of fish this time."

Valentinian glanced up at her inscrutably. He was a nice-looking kid, if she wanted to pursue a cougar fantasy. Alternatively, Dave appeared to be almost as old as her father.

But both kept a respectable distance. From her and everyone else. Lianearia supposed that the call girls at the next planet might get a workout, if the two men were pent up with celibacy.

Or perhaps she might have a chat with the cook.

Best to keep everyone happy.

[7]

VALENTINIAN

VALENTINIAN DIDN'T BOTHER STOPPING as they passed through the dining hall, on the way to the starboard engine nacelle. He glanced back when he felt Dave pause, but the big man caught up fast enough.

Around them, all nine girls were heads down, writing on paper supplied by Cleray, silent and intent.

"What was that?" Dave whispered as they got to the far end of the hallway, opened the engine nacelle, and crowded in.

There was just enough space here for the two of them and a toolbox, as long as nobody moved suddenly. With the hatch closed, they could talk in low voices.

"Accounting homework," Valentinian replied, just as quietly.

"What?" Dave reared back and bonked his head on an overhead pipe. "Ow."

"Yeah, don't do that," Valentinian grinned up at him. "I'm short enough to pass below the overhead stuff."

"Accounting?" Dave asked again, rubbing the crown of his skull.

"I asked Hiranur," Valentinian replied. "Apparently, on top of all the dancing and singing, Madame Cleray makes them take classes in languages, business, and accounting. Something about being prepared for a second career after Solaria Femina."

"Interesting." Dave knelt this time, rather than squatting in the space. "So she's not just another mogul exploiting innocents?"

"Not just, would be my take," Valentinian said. "They've any of them got like maybe five years, tops, for the youngest ones. Cleray *was* them, once. She's rich now, and trying to sustain this, and apparently making sure she has a clean conscience."

"How'd she end up with you?" Dave teased.

Valentinian had told the man enough of his background for Dave to be able to pretend to have been a crewmember longer than this trip, in case anybody asked. That included his time at Gymnasia Dominia, and the fallout and issues that left him here.

Including the poker night he stumbled into that got him the stake to buy this ship.

Valentinian grinned at the memory.

Look around the poker table. If you can't identify the mark, then it's you.

Fortunately, it had been someone else that time. And the wolves fleecing the sheep hadn't even minded Valentinian raking off a nice pot towards the end. Right before they stripped that bastard of everything, including the shirt off his back.

Valentinian had folded with a High Stack/Low Stack as the bidding climbed, knowing that the hammer was about to drop. The mark had been sitting on a Mixed Pyramid, and betting crazy amounts.

Dumbass.

Valentinian had happily, gratefully walked away when things had gotten heated as someone else beat the mark with only the second Perfect Arcade Valentinian had ever seen. Right before the mark tried to get ugly.

As if men and women like that wouldn't have planned for violence.

Longshot Hypothesis had been the outcome.

"The Creator watches out for angels and fools," Valentinian smiled up at the big guy.

"You're supposed to be an angel, now?" Dave laughed.

"Something like that," Valentinian laughed back.

He tried, anyways.

Honest and ethical were two entirely different things, regardless of how close they were supposed to be. He didn't scam or steal from anyone that couldn't afford it. And didn't take advantage of the ones that couldn't.

Close enough to an angel, he supposed.

"So what happens when we get to Aestrolathia," Dave asked. "I've never been there."

Valentinian shrugged, sobering. He pulled out the electric impact hammer and opened up a panel to expose the feed lines and filters inside.

"It's a boring kind of world, for the most part," he said. "Heavy on farming and ranching. They ship grain and meat elsewhere at a profit, but the people are mostly farmers. The bankers are pretty restrained, since the High Street flash is back on Cronus Prime. But they'll go in for pretty, teenage girls in tight, skimpy outfits, doing synchronized sex appeal."

"And if Nash shows up?" Dave got serious. "Do we know what he's about?"

"I'll be wearing a shock pistol the entire time I'm on the ground," Valentinian felt the growl start in his stomach. "You will as well. If they start something, we'll finish it. I'm happy to go back and have someone review the tapes from Dominion Prime. They started it and threw the first punch."

"And if he's got official friends here?" Dave growled back. "Gendarmes willing to look the other way, or prosecutors on the take?"

"I'd happily send an anonymous tip to that White Hat that inspected us before we left," Valentinian said. "It would be fun, watching her bounce Nash and his people off bulkheads when they got salty at her."

"Yeah," Dave agreed. "But I'd rather we never saw White Hats again."

"With you there," Valentinian said. "That one frightens me in ways no cop ever has. Not sure even Laurentia would be far enough away to escape her, if she got it in her mind to come after us."

Dave grew quiet. Valentinian poked his head into the gap and checked all the indicators.

"Okay, look here, here, and here," Valentinian continued, pointing. "This is what a normal feed line looks like. You'll see the markers go yellow initially, when they need to be cleaned or replaced. After that, red or black indicates a blockage and probable failure that requires the engine be taken apart, so you'll need to check these about every three days when we're in warp, and weekly otherwise. Don't try to fix anything for now. Just let me know and I'll show you how to take it all apart. The Anuradhans did weird things with their sublight drives. Maybe more efficient than Dominion tech, but bigger too, and damned near backwards."

"Got it," Dave said. "So would you really go beyond mapped space?"

"Huh?" Valentinian turned to look at the man, sensing some restrained hope in the man. Like that would make Dave's day. "Oh, White Hats. Maybe. Her chasing us? I'd hit Wildspace in a heartbeat. Nash doesn't frighten me. He's just a bully boy. Pretty sure he'll try something stupid at Aestrolathia, but that's only because he'll hire muscle on site, and they won't be told about what happened to the last batch of dumbasses."

"Should I carry a blade?" Dave asked in a tight, serious voice.

Valentinian carried a blade with him everywhere. Well, a pocket multi-tool, but that wasn't what Dave was asking. He meant a big one. A meter of steel with a killing edge, in the hands of someone who knew how to use it.

The emblem of the crazy folks that joined the Dominion and served in the Caelons or other brigades.

Valentinian had never had to deal with those armored goons that made up the Dominion's Assault Cavalry, but everybody knew the plate mail they wore. The heavy blaster on a sling.

The hand-and-a-half sword hanging over one shoulder.

Yeah, Valentinian knew what he meant.

On the one hand, *nobody* would mess with the man if Dave had a sword on a baldric. On the other hand, nobody would have the least doubts who Dave was, or had been.

Someone would start asking questions, and Valentinian was pretty sure he didn't want to know the answers.

"No," Valentinian decided. "That's just asking for trouble. Especially if you end up having to cut someone in half to make a point. And you would. But I have an idea."

"Tell me," Dave commanded in a voice that was suddenly less solicitous.

That sounded more like the man Dave had been a month ago, Valentinian decided. An officer of some sort, probably. Wearing a mask, like all the rest of the Dominion's elite troopers.

"So we start with a metal tube, about three decimeters long," Valentinian said. "Something light and tough, with a high ductile strength. Then we machine a second tube, just enough smaller that it will fit inside the first, and flare one end out with a ram or something. Same with a third piece, except we weld or screw a small ball of steel at the end, maybe with lead inside."

"A telescoping baton," Dave snapped his fingers. His eyes lit up with excitement. "Yes, concealable, but still lets me fight like I held my…sword. And not kill people, but settle for breaking bones. I could make something like that with the equipment in the machine shop."

"You can?" Valentinian had been expecting to have to do the machine work himself.

Of course a militant warrior berserker monk would know how to make weapons.

And Valentinian had caught the pause. Every order, every discipline, every heritage called their sword by a different term. Had Dave used it here, Valentinian could have looked it up later and known where the man came from.

And Dave grinned in a lopsided way at him as they both realized it.

"As soon as we're done here, I'll start looking at piping," Dave offered. "I've never made one, but I understand the theory. Shouldn't take more than a day. And close combat with blades is so much more personal than just shooting someone with a shock pistol."

Valentinian grunted and let that one go. He'd only shot someone twice, and neither time had required more than a demonstration of willingness to shoot.

Bar fights were a whole other thing, and shatterproof beer pitchers were still his weapon of choice there. Useful defensively as well, if you could get some drunk to punch a pitcher with an uncovered fist to break bones in his hand.

"So now, let's move on to the sensors in the engine, and how to test and adjust them…" Valentinian said.

[8]
KYRIAKI

Kyriaki had only been in the Ambassador's office on two other occasions, one of which had been her first joining this team, and the second for a commendation awarded for hard work.

Neither sounded to be on the schedule today.

Three weeks had aged the Ambassador a decade, it seemed. The lines were carved deeper, as though by earth-shattering spring floods.

She sat across from the desk from him carefully still and waiting.

"There have been no new leads in the investigation of the Dominator's death," he said gravely. "His assassination. We know the event occurred on this station, and that no unaccounted-for person was able to depart in the week following."

She nodded. They had stepped up the paranoia, going so far as to break small-time criminal enterprises that had been left alone previously. It was always better to watch and take names against later charges, rather than to immediately shatter an organization and perhaps miss the big fish swimming away in the confusion.

But she had been ruthless. As had her fellows.

"Either the assassin never left the station, which we doubt, or managed the perfect escape," the Ambassador continued. "I have reviewed your files of the transport *Longshot Hypothesis*, and its captain, Valentinian Tarasicodissa. And I agree with you that it is a thin thread to pursue, perhaps even stochastically meaningless. We may see a pattern where there is none, merely because we wish to see one."

He paused and rubbed his bald head for a moment, showing the enormous strain.

The Ambassador felt as if he had personally failed. She could see that in his face. As if the White Hats had failed, even though guarding the Dominator was not their responsibility. Catching his killer should be.

"In addition," the man continued in a harder, colder voice. "I have reviewed older files on Tarasicodissa that you have not been privy to. Three years ago, he was banished from the Gymnasia Dominia for ethical irregularities. The file has very carefully been sanitized, but I suspect he was made a scapegoat for others who escaped punishment. We cannot tell, without interviewing certain members of the elite who I do not wish to antagonize without a greater level of evidence."

He stopped there. Studied her face with eyes like a hungry owl emerging from the darkness.

"With no other avenues, I am reduced to the worst. To grasping at straws, Inspector," he confided in a quiet voice that frightened Kyriaki more than anything she had encountered in years.

"Sir?" she asked, trying to keep her own nerves in check, lest they color her tone in an accusatory manner.

"We have reached a dead end, Kyriaki," he admitted. "There will be a new Dominator in far too short a time, once the Tournament of Domination concludes. I wish to present something other than failure to our new lord upon their ascension."

"How may I serve?" She suddenly felt like a small fish in a very deep and dark ocean, while ominous things swam by hungrily below.

Kyriaki had always been intense and driven. It got her here. Put her in the white beret. Made her a respected officer.

But now she might be brought to the attention of a new Dominator, and do so as a representative of their collective failure.

Messengers had been killed for less.

"I am assigning you to a new mission, Inspector," the Ambassador rasped. "You will be on detached duty starting immediately. I would rather be a fool than a coward, Kyriaki, so you will investigate Tarasicodissa and his current mission. There are holes in his paperwork and records that suggest someone at a very high level has been manipulating circumstances in subtle and effective ways. I do not like it, but we lack the evidence to challenge the Solar Party on this. At least so far."

"Pursue *Longshot Hypothesis*?" she pressed with the faintest hope in her eyes. "And then what?"

Even she knew that trumped-up charges would fall apart at the first hearing, unless she uncovered a serious plot against the Dominion. The kind that might never make it to an open hearing because the conspirators needed to be killed rather than being taken alive.

"Dig, Kyriaki," the man ordered harshly. "Find out why Solaria Femina suddenly broke with their previous transport and partners, right before all this happened, and came to hire Tarasicodissa instead. Determine where a family-less youth without legitimate employment acquired the funds to buy his ship less than three months after being thrown out of the Gymnasia. Identify his friends and backers, so that we might have further avenues to pursue. Give me something we can show to our new Dominator that we take their safety seriously. None of it adds up to treason, as far as I can tell, even with hindsight, but it also does not amount to nothing."

"And if I fail to uncover the plot we suspect?" she asked carefully.

"There may have never been one, Inspector," the Ambassador grew warmer. "Occasionally, chaos appears patterned, at least for an instant, before collapsing again. Like a soap bubble on a spring day. A conspiracy that big and sophisticated should have left more evidence behind, unless it was at the highest levels. You will not have failed, if you do, for lack of diligence. That is why I chose you over any of the other officers."

Kyriaki actually blushed at the left-handed compliment from her ultimate superior. She had years before she was eligible to be promoted to Inquisitor, unless she broke a major case open. Like this one might become.

Perhaps she might even need to manufacture a little of the evidence she needed. Tarasicodissa was not clean. It would just be a matter of using the right leverage on the man. Or his compatriots.

"I will make you proud, Ambassador," she said, standing.

He stood as well, reaching forward to shake her hand.

"Find me the truth, Inspector," he countered.

She would.

Or she would at least find a way to deliver Tarasicodissa's head on a stake.

VALENTINIAN

VALENTINIAN WATCHED the station as they got close for docking, following all the correct navigational instructions like a good, little merchant. *Longshot Hypothesis* was running at about ten percent power, where most ships this size would be decelerating into orbit at about a third of their total drive capacity. But they didn't have engines as big as he did, either.

Aestrolathia was a dull and dreary planet that had never inspired Valentinian to stay longer than necessary to deliver a cargo or passenger to an orbital station, or a landing pad; find his next cargo run; and then leave.

But if he was going to be here a while, and he suspected they were, he'd survive.

The people here were nice enough, after all, in a restricted, farmerly sort of way. All they cared about, most of the time, were futures contracts, weather forecasts, and currency fluctuations. A few occasionally had daughters that broke loose from the pack and ran away, looking for excitement. Usually, they eventually ended up someplace like Jnini Centra, to be sucked into the vortex of beautiful people and the monsters that preyed on them.

All the while dreaming of being a vid star.

Plus sporadically, you had middle-aged housewives looking for a little adventure on the side.

Valentinian wasn't too concerned that he would have to undertake an extended case of monasticism on Aestrolathia, even if he was surrounded, twenty-six hours a day/eight days a week, by beautiful girls. Most of them were so utterly focused on dancing, singing, and homework that he doubted any of them even knew his name.

He had been introduced, early on, but hadn't bothered associating names with faces. Even if he could. At best, each girl could be tracked by the color their hair had been dyed, and the particular cut, as the only way to tell them apart. Madame Cleray had chosen them to be identical. Music videos focused on that similarity, balanced by just enough difference to keep you interested.

More or less.

"Aestrolathia Flight Control, this is *Longshot Hypothesis*, on final approach," Valentinian said into the radio as the hatch behind him opened and Dave entered, taking the starboard seat.

"Acknowledged, *Longshot Hypothesis*," the man's voice came back, sharp and even professional. "Docking bay B-23 still cleared and awaiting docking. No secondary services have been engaged at this time. Is that correct?"

"Affirmative, Control," Valentinian said. "Passengers may debark temporarily before returning, and we'll need to arrange to take on supplies later. I'm hauling the musical group Solaria Femina for shows on the station and the ground."

"Roger that," the man perked up. Apparently he had heard of them. Or maybe just anything new was good for a smile. "Customs will meet you shortly."

And the line was closed.

"Customs?" Dave asked in a careful, trying-to-sound-casual tone.

"Standard operating procedure," Valentinian assured his new first mate, a man who had obviously never done this before, but was willing to learn.

Because, you know, even crazed, warrior monks can have mid-life crises.

"What happens?" Dave pressed, obviously at a loss.

Have you never flown commercial, dude?

"So we back into the station and dock, just like at Dominion Prime," Valentinian explained. "Two officials come aboard and check everyone's papers against a central registry. In your case, they'll add you, but I've already been here a few times. Since we don't have cargo, they don't have to check the manifest and make sure I have all the right buttons stuck on."

"What did he mean about secondary services?" Dave's face scrunched up in concentration.

"No cargo being delivered, so I don't need stevedores or pipeline services, beyond just docking to the station and drawing air, water, and power from there for a few days," Valentinian said. "We're flying this about as casual as possible, just waiting for that bully Nash to start something, either here, which I doubt, or down on the planet, where it will be harder for gendarmes to track things."

"Okay," Dave nodded.

The big man was more nervous that the situation warranted. But Dave probably expected whatever trouble he had fled, back on Dominion Prime, would catch up with him, and be waiting on the dock when they arrived.

Valentinian hadn't explained just how fast the warp bubble this ship could generate was, or how hard he had pushed to get here ahead of anybody else's news.

Even the fastest military couriers, running flat out, would

have had to start almost at the same time, just to beat them here by a few hours. At least this time.

Valentinian wasn't showing off, so much as fleeing the scene of a crime he didn't even know about, on the safe assumption that Dave needed to be elsewhere, and in a hurry.

Because the last thing Valentinian wanted was to be collateral damage if somebody felt the need to arrest the big man.

He opened the internal comm and broadcast everywhere, since he didn't want to try to figure out where the woman was right now. Not on his command deck, and that was good enough.

"Madame Cleray, this is your captain," he announced. "We'll be docking with the station and ready for customs inspection in approximately one hour."

A pause. Probably her getting over her shock.

"We're more than a day ahead of schedule, Valentinian," she replied from the lounge.

"Yes, ma'am," he shared a grin with Dave as he spoke. "I hope that won't be a problem?"

"No, no," she even sounded excited. "This gives us time to perhaps add in extra performances. I will have everyone ready."

Valentinian cut the line and settled back. The flight path was programmed, and the ship could pretty much dock itself at this point. He needed to be ready for emergencies, surprises, and idiots not obeying traffic lanes in space.

Dave still looked concerned.

"We're really a day early?" he asked hesitantly.

"There is the *slightest* chance that news from Dominion Prime got here ahead of us," Valentinian suggested. "If they pushed and had a ship as fast as mine. Most don't, and regular news will take a week, unless something crazy happened, right about the time we were leaving."

Dave's face revealed nothing. Not the slightest emotional signature.

Which suggested the man had just drawn an Inside Perfect Arcade on his last card.

Something big must have happened back there. And Valentinian was doubly sure today that he didn't want to know, certainly not from Dave, just in case he ended up having to testify later.

Your Excellency, the first time I heard that my new first mate might be a criminal was when he was arrested. I am just as shocked and appalled as the rest of you…

Or something like that.

Maybe not that bad, since Dave had saved him from getting his ass kicked by Nash and friends. And might do so again.

But yeah, honesty would look so much better, if Valentinian was called to testify.

Dave wanted to say something. Valentinian would have nothing to do with it, so he called up a short-range scan on the screen between them and began to fiddle with it, just to stop looking at the big man, and whatever demons he was exercising today.

Valentinian suspected that something big would be all over the local news boards, probably in about two days.

[10]
LIANEARIA

LIANEARIA HAD NOT BEEN able to sleep. Not that she was surprised. She had always managed to get by on four to six hours of sleep per night. Less in an emergency, but nothing untoward had happened.

The station where they had docked yesterday kept time with Dominion Prime, just like the ship did, so her internal clock was still synchronized. It was extremely early in the morning.

If they were at their next destination on the surface of the planet below, the sun would just now be thinking about rising soon. Roosters would still be warm and content, assuming no foxes had come sniffing about.

But her mind was fully awake. And her body quickly joined it.

The girls were asleep yet. Even Hiranur would only now be thinking about getting out of her warm bed and preparing breakfast for everyone.

Lianearia had grown restless, almost manic this morning, for reasons she could not identify. So she rose and made her way to the kitchen. Fixed a mug of strong tea as a way to calm her nerves and sensibilities.

A sound echoed up the stairwell to her as she sat in the kitchen and sipped. A hatch opening below.

Intrigued, she silently glided to the top of the stairs on bare feet, stopping to put a cap on her tea mug before ghosting down to the landing, pausing to peek around the corner at the lights below.

During ship's night, the captain normally kept the overheads at the lowest setting, just enough that someone could find their way to the kitchen or head without their own flashlight.

Down in engineering, a light spilled into the engineering hallway from beyond. Someone was in the cargo bay, and had brought those lights up halfway.

Lianearia squatted down to try to see who it was. She assumed one of the girls had risen earlier than the rest and was down in the big space practicing her steps. But from here, the angle was wrong. She could only see a shadow moving.

Carefully, she slid against the outer edge of the staircase, out of view of the open doors to the cargo bay. She would want to know who was working extra hard in secrecy, either because the girl deserved a gold star, or because she was behind her sisters and needed to be worked harder, or perhaps considered for replacement.

Music was a cruel and unforgiving business. Even Lianearia had to cull them with a farmer's eye, if she wanted to maintain the reputation of Solaria Femina for another decade or more.

Into the engineering space hallway she slipped, still unable to see beyond, or hear whoever was moving about.

Closer she crept, staying against the wall on her left.

She could hear footsteps now, the slap of gripping soles against the metal deck, almost inaudible.

Lianearia was impressed. Most of the girls made far more noise when dancing, since the music covered it. Someone was going through her steps in near-perfect silence.

Moving like sap from a cold tree, she peeked barely an eye around the sill to spy within the cargo bay.

Her gasp was hopefully silent, because it wasn't Meryem or Belinay practicing.

The First Mate was moving in a slow-elaborate dance of his own.

Fortunately, he had his back to her as she slipped back out of sight, but she had studied enough martial arts in her dancing to recognize the man's movements. And her Dancemaster, Kostantina, had served in the Solar Guard for a time, teaching the girls additional classes in self-defense, to go with learning how to walk and dance.

The giant man moved with a grace and power at least as good as any woman Lianearia had ever seen dance.

She pressed herself against the wall and slid away from the door as quietly as humanly possible.

The man had been moving with a length of pipe in both hands, slashing and blocking invisible opponents in the slow, deliberate steps of kata training.

Muscle memory.

Once you embedded the moves, you could bring them out at a much greater speed, slashing and killing on a real battleground at a speed almost too quickly to see.

Lianearia could fight, with or without weapons. She lacked the brute strength or mass of that man, but she suspected from the way he moved that he was faster in combat than she was, something she had not seen during the fight in the bar, as she was occupied at the time.

But Hall had engaged four or five men and taken them

all down so quickly that it was almost a blur, even in her memory.

Quickly, she retraced her silent steps, anxious to be upstairs and away from the man before he realized that he had entertained an audience who could appreciate his moves.

Kostantina had showed her some of the same moves, to be used with a dancing sword, but Lianearia had not incorporated them into any song recently. Nothing she had written had suggested that level of martial splendor.

But Lianearia still recognized the katas. The Dominator's Caelons, the elite shock troops of the Dominion itself, trained that way.

Who was this man Hall?

[11]

VALENTINIAN

FOR A STATION that excelled at being bright and clean, Valentinian was amazed at how dark and grungy the doorway in front of him was. The proprietor had to work really hard, just to make a bar feel like such a dive.

Probably got fines from the station and intentionally racked up health code violations in the kitchen, just to maintain the ambiance. The air inside stank of smoke and old grease, in spite of being on a space station.

"Is it safe?" he heard Dave rumble, a step behind him.

"Seriously?" Valentinian glanced back as his eyes began to adjust to the gloom.

"Hey, last time I was in a bar with you, I had to beat the place up," Dave noted with a wry grin. "Just managing expectations."

"Very funny," Valentinian replied grumpily.

He got deeper into the bar and kept his thoughts to himself. Dave had never been to Aestrolathia. It was an out-of-the-way place that usually dealt with mega-freighters from the big houses, hauling in cargo loads bigger than all of *Longshot Hypothesis* herself.

At least the man was relaxing. Trying to fit in. Pretending to be a spacer, instead of whatever it was he had been two months ago. Or a year ago.

However long had to pass from the moment a man woke up disgusted with the sum of his life's choices, to the point he chucked it all out the airlock and started over.

Valentinian found a table along a side wall, farthest away from the smoke signals being generated in the kitchen. Not that it made much difference, but it made him feel better.

"This is business, so I'm buying drinks," he muttered to Dave as they sat.

At least everyone in here was human, as near as he could tell in the gloom and hoods up around heads. That would change if they left the Dominion for some of the weirder neighbors. The Dominion was still a human-centric place.

"I have money cached," Dave got serious. "Not enough that they'll miss it, but more than enough to keep me going for several years."

Valentinian didn't ask who *they* were. Not that he figured Dave would actually tell the truth, but anything that left him a fool rather than an accomplice was better, on the day when Dave's past inevitably caught up with them.

Valentinian was betting on the wife making an appearance. As the waitress took their orders and headed back to the bar, Valentinian amused himself with trying to imagine the woman Dave would have married. Or the kids, since Dave had mentioned that he had a boy and a girl about Valentinian's own age.

It was pointless, but fun. More likely, a squad of Caelons, in full assault armor, would suddenly walk into the bar with guns pointed at the two of them, and they'd end up in a jail cell, eventually on Dominion Prime.

Valentinian had no idea what sorts of torture might be acceptable, once they had Dave in their hands, but even the best truth serum couldn't get anything out of Valentinian, if he didn't know it.

Cowardice has many forms. This was the one Valentinian knew he could handle, looking in the mirror. And yeah, he was probably looking at himself in another twenty-five years, seated across the table, so he could at least prepare well for his own mid-life crisis.

He wondered how he'd look in monastic robes with a shaved head as the drinks got delivered.

"Why are we here, anyway?" Dave's silence finally cracked as the waitress delivered two glasses of something amber, took coin, and left.

"Looking for a man," Valentinian replied quietly. "Don't know who he is, what his name might be, or what he looks like, so I'm hoping he finds me, eventually."

"Was that supposed to make any sense?" Dave asked.

"The local fixer," Valentinian clarified. "The guy who finds things for you that aren't necessarily listed in a business catalog somewhere."

He watched Dave's eyes grow distant for a moment. Judgmental, perhaps, but the big man kept his mouth shut. Something about having previously been a songbird in a pretty cage must have registered on the fellow, because his eyes changed and the grin came back.

"I have had it easy, haven't I?" he asked.

"That's why I'm the captain, and you're the first mate," Valentinian grinned back. "You're too wet behind the ears to be safe out on your own just yet."

Dave lapsed into silence and sipped. Valentinian did the same, enjoying the smoky flavor of the beer. Like all bars everywhere, tail ends of casks and leftovers were mixed in a central tank and served to anyone asking. It was always a mixed bag, what flavor you might end up with, but it tended down into the brown, porter range, and was cheap, if you wanted alcohol and weren't too pissy about being a beer snob.

Valentinian could have afforded the good stuff. Just didn't want to get into that habit. A Solar not spent on beer was available later for maintenance, or went into the retirement fund, where it would make more with the magic of compounding interest.

You had to take the long view on these things.

An old man approached, wearing weird robes that combined the classical monk with some desert sensibilities. Inquiring with them about transport to the sector capital for himself and a nephew.

Valentinian didn't like the look of the old man. Smelled like trouble. More trouble. Dominion-troops-getting-involved kind of trouble. He took a hard pass. Watched the man return to the bar itself.

A fight broke out when the old man got there. Someone didn't like the kid. Flamers got pulled out. Valentinian watched a sword appear from under those robes. Someone lost an arm and the troublemakers were suddenly running for their lives, and presumably the nearest medical facility.

Dave had tensed. Valentinian could almost smell the energy coming off the big man as the fracas settled itself over there.

"We're out of here," he decided, leaving the other half of his beer on the table and standing.

Dave looked up at him in surprise.

"Why?" he asked, confused.

"Weapons means someone is going to call the cops," Valentinian explained. "Even here. Probably send Caelons down here, considering which bar it was. I don't want to be questioned and possibly detained, since the old man might have been seen talking to us. Let's go."

Dave shrugged and nodded. He slid out of the booth and

stood up to his immense height, glowering unconsciously at everyone and everything in here.

Across the bar, Valentinian watched the old man sit down at another table. Another pair of spacers, one human and one a tall, furry alien, looked just as disreputable as Valentinian felt right now. He could always come back later.

After whatever other trouble was brewing with that old man blew past.

Out in the hallway, Valentinian considered his options. The station was a big torus, flattened into three oversized decks and spinning slowly on its axis as it orbited the planet below. This was the commercial deck. Above them it was mostly residential, where the permanent inhabitants lived. Below was the industrial area, where the on-station manufacturing took place.

Valentinian took a look back at the dim interior of the space, and made sure Dave was close at hand, as he flipped a coin in his head and turned left. He did enough work on the elliptical machine that he was in good shape. Could probably circumnavigate the station a couple of times if he needed to, but he didn't want to go far.

This was the rougher neighborhood, as it were. The spacer bars that were kept as far away from the tourist spaces as possible, just like on nearly every station he had ever docked. It worked better that way, for everyone.

Still, he wanted to appear to be more of a law-abiding type, rather than someone with a bounty on his head, fleeing ahead of the cops, so he picked a coffee house down a few doors and across the promenade. Inside, he ordered a small pot of tea and settled himself in to let it steep.

Because they were close to the open front door, Valentinian watched the front and sat Dave in such a way that the big man could see the interior. Not ideal, but something about coffee shops seemed to preclude fights, for the most part. Valentinian presumed there was a science behind it. Probably something to do with alcohol versus caffeine. Getting wound up as opposed to trying to relax.

Time passed. Tea steeped. Dave watched. Valentinian noted the arrival of four goons in white and orange battle armor across the way, plus a man in a severe, black uniform.

Caelons, just like he had expected.

They emerged a few minutes later, none the wiser, but Valentinian had already watched the old man and his nephew slink out the door and vanish down the walkway beforehand.

Creator only knew what kind of trouble that old man was. Far worse than Madame Cleray. Hopefully Dave would end up being a sheep in wolves' clothing, a runaway accountant when all was said and done, and Valentinian was just over-sensitive.

A guy can hope, right?

Another man stepped to the doorway, paused, looked around. He smiled at Valentinian in a manner so oily Valentinian wondered if a shower would be necessary to get the smell out later.

The stranger approached, hands stretched across an ample gut barely contained by a silk scarf wrapped around his middle several times. The bald head and beady eyes might have come out of a casting catalog. The clothing was expensive, if mismatched. Valentinian wondered if the man normally looked like that, and had been pressed into the arena, or had cultivated the image that everyone expected when he got there.

"May I?" he indicated the empty chair on the side.

"Indeed," Valentinian smiled with his teeth but not his eyes. "The tea approaches perfection. Surely, I can impose upon you to join us in having a cup?"

"I would be delighted to assist," the man said, sitting as the old ritual greeting was completed.

"Valentinian," he introduced himself to the used-speeder-dealer as he poured a third mug and slid it across the table to the man.

"Ahdramenites," the man answered, taking a polite sip as Valentinian did. "I might have noticed you in a bar, recently."

Valentinian shrugged.

"We were approached about a charter, but my crew cabins are already booked for the foreseeable future," Valentinian replied. "And that old man asking was Dominion trouble awaiting the axe. I have better ways to spend my life."

"So I concluded as well," the fixer replied, his smile as slick and transparent as his manner. "What brings you to Aestrolathia, gentlemen?"

"Our charter," Valentinian said simply. "Her itinerary has many worlds and stops. We are the tour bus for Solaria Femina for the time being."

"Indeed?" the man's eyebrows climbed up to his non-existent scalp. "May we all be so lucky as to spend our days surrounded by such beautiful women."

"You know them?" Valentinian inquired. And noticed the ghost of a fist clenching on Dave's hand as he drank his own tea.

Big guy didn't like the stranger much more than Valentinian did, but you had to build pyramids with the cards you were dealt.

"They have traveled to our planet with regularity," Ahdramenites smiled.

"Then perhaps you know Madame Cleray's former partner. A gentleman named Nash, I believe?" Valentinian decided to play the innocent today.

He watched the man's eyes like they had both just gone

all in on the pot between them. Noted the flicker that the man didn't suppress fast enough, the slight moue of distaste that never was more than a suggestion of a hint.

"I might have encountered the man, it is possible," Ahdramenites allowed. "Could you describe him?"

Valentinian did, leaving out the parts where the fight had broken out and Dave had shown himself to be another one of those dangerous, warrior monks, like the old man across the way. No reason to frighten this font of information.

At least, not yet.

"Ah, yes," Ahdramenites smiled politely. "I may have indeed met him. But, of course, I have not seen him lately."

Valentinian reached into a pocket of his jacket and palmed a coin. Reaching out, he placed it across the table silently in front of the stranger.

"We would, of course, like to avoid any misunderstandings with the man," Valentinian said as he withdrew his empty hand. "Perhaps if he followed us here, you might hear news of it before we did, and let us know?"

The hand moved like a striking snake on a lively mouse, swallowing the coin in a blur.

"I will keep my eyes and ears open, gentleman," he smiled, just as oily. "Is there other business we might transact at the current time?"

"There might be," Valentinian let his word trail off. "I believe Madame Cleray's next stop is down on the planet below, so we will need to research things like a central landing pad for my ship, ground transport for the women, and possibly lodging, since they may choose to spend a few nights closer to their theater, rather than running back and forth to the ship each night. Do you have any friends on the surface that might be beneficial to call?"

"I can do you so much better," the man's eyes lit up. "I have a cousin."

Valentinian smiled. They all had cousins. If you listened close enough, every fixer on every planet and station was actually part of one extended clan, rather than just belonging to a thieves guild with membership cards.

But that was how business worked. One man's hustle turned into connections and favors flowing about. Aestrolathia was a new world to Valentinian, at least for staying this long, and there was no reason he might not be back this way at some point.

Assuming that Dave's problems weren't so great that all of them ended up running for Wildspace as fast and as hard as they could.

"You are the captain of *Longshot Hypothesis*?" Ahdramenites asked tentatively.

Valentinian hadn't mentioned his ship at any point, but he wasn't surprised the man had done his homework. He had come looking for them, after all.

"I am," Valentinian nodded and pointed to the big, mean, bastard of a warrior monk daintily sipping tea across from him. "My first mate, Dave."

"Charmed," Dave actually set his mug down and shook the man's hand.

Ahdramenites's eyes lit up as he no doubt felt the callouses that developed when you held a sword enough. A different calculation took shape in an eyeblink.

"Let me call my cousin and make inquiries," he propositioned. "So that whatever Madame Cleray's needs are, we can immediately meet them."

"I look forward to your message, Ahdramenites," Valentinian smiled as the man rose.

"Until then."

And he was gone.

"How did that go?" Dave asked tentatively after the man vanished.

"About as well as could be expected," Valentinian replied. "He knew who we were before he walked in. Now he knows we'll do business and want a long-term thing, so he's evaluating where this puts Nash and how many favors are on the abacus right now. And I'm pretty sure he realized at the end just how dangerous you could be, so he has to add that to the scale."

"Exactly as intended," Dave smiled. "You seemed to have it in hand, but half of what you said was gibberish to me."

"We'll make a spacer out of you yet," Valentinian finished his tea and stood with a warm smile. "Now, let's head back to the nicer parts of the station and find a shop. I have a few needs, and then I want dinner."

Dave rose and followed, glancing about as if he suspected he was being watched.

Valentinian knew they were under observation. He just didn't know who the watchers were going to tell.

Or how much trouble that would bring.

[12]

VALENTINIAN

AT NO POINT had Valentinian mentioned his previous itinerary, but he supposed that Madame Cleray's schedule was public knowledge, if you were into that sort of thing, so people might know that they had come here directly from Dominion Prime.

And left just before news had emerged that the Dominator, the old Dominator, had been assassinated, suddenly and effectively.

Little was known publically about the upper echelons of the Solar Party and the capstone of the Dominion government himself. Valentinian supposed Qetesh Intelligence, or maybe Lei-Zu would have insights, but he was just a spacer.

So he played it as stupid as a sheep when the news exploded and every broadsheet on every table over breakfast had every dribble of news available that their sovereign lord and master was dead. Ignored the people around him when they chattered back and forth around him as breakfast was ending. And even more columns of talk were dedicated to handicapping the sudden entrants who might be admitted into the Tournament of Domination that would culminate in the next ruler.

All the news was at least two weeks out of date anyway, so nobody could do more than speculate. And Valentinian really didn't want to take a guess at the timing that had him here.

Too much chance of truth serum in his future.

Especially now.

At least most of the information was held as a state secret. Timing wouldn't tell anybody anything, especially since he could honestly say that the last person he talked to before he left Dominion Prime was one of the White Hats. And he would, if asked.

Anything to maintain *stupid*.

They were down on the surface of Aestrolathia today, having landed last night, probably about the same time that a courier dropped out of warp with the official news, once the government felt it needed to tell the population. The spies around here had probably learned just about as fast as *Longshot Hypothesis* had originally gotten here.

At least nobody had come to talk to him.

Valentinian was late to breakfast for the usual crowd. Right at the tail end, just before brunch people would have started to wander in. The starport where they had docked had indeed belonged to a cousin of Ahdramenites, more or less, but it was centrally located, close to the main transit hubs, and the rates were good enough.

Plus, the restaurant specialized in what they called a farmer breakfast, served all day. Heavy on carbs and meat, slathered over with gravy at the slightest excuse. Hiranur's cooking was fantastic, but she was absolutely dedicated to keeping young girls svelte and healthy.

Sometimes a man needed drop-biscuits covered with

sausage gravy and cheese, plus a couple liters of black coffee, to start his day.

Valentinian had let Dave sleep in, the planetary clock being offset some from the ship, but the man was up and walked in looking like he had just run fifteen kilometers and showered afterwards.

Valentinian considered hating him on general principles, but Dave was a good guy, as near as he could tell. Or a good enough actor to make up for it. And that was all that really mattered.

The big man sauntered over like he had been practicing his public walk. He might have. Most of the time, he looked like he was grimly headed up the hill to kick in the door and kill everyone in the tower. Today was rather mellow, so he hadn't heard the news yet.

Valentinian waved a half-empty coffee mug at Dave as he continued to shovel over-easy eggs and cooked potatoes into his mouth. The news broadsheet could wait. There was nothing in there Valentinian hadn't heard already.

Dave sat, glancing at the page. He stopped and blanched, turning white for a moment.

Valentinian put his coffee down momentarily and slid the paper across to the man, making eye contact with the waiter. The big man would want food and coffee to deal with the shock.

Or at least to have time to refine whatever cover story he was going to tell.

"And what can I get you to drink this morning?" the waiter asked solicitously as he walked up.

Dave had fallen silent when Valentinian looked over.

"He'll need coffee, and a menu," Valentinian offered.

"Right away." And he was gone.

Valentinian was finished with his food about the time Dave finished reading the second page article that offered nothing more relevant than the best place to place bets on the various stages of the Tournament. A lot of money was going to change hands soon.

"Huh," Dave even managed to sound convincing, in case any strangers happened to be listening in.

The joint was mostly empty right now, but the next crop of folks was just making their way across the landing field. The sun had only been up for about an hour, and nobody but ranchers got up early on Aestrolathia, apparently.

"Just glad we got out when we did," Valentinian replied in a vague voice. "Apparently, they shut down all transit about four hours after we got clear of the station. Didn't start clearing people for about three days. Last any news came in, nothing new about the assassin, or how he did it."

Long pause from the big guy. Digesting. Re-calculating.

Ignorance would be no defense now, if Dave was that kind of killer. Valentinian and probably even Madame Cleray would be thrown into small, dark cells and left to sweat. Possibly just executed out of spite.

Hopefully, she was smart enough to realize that, and keep her own mouth shut. And not let her girls or staff talk to anybody outside the ship.

"So now what?" Dave asked innocently.

Valentinian shrugged.

"Unless you feel the need to race back to Dominion Prime, so that you can add your name to the list of people wanting to vie for ultimate power, I don't see how anything changes," Valentinian replied. "I have a charter contract with Madame Cleray. You've got an employment contract as first mate, unless you want to break it."

He turned innocent eyes on Dave, daring the man to break character for long enough to come clean and get them all executed. Valentinian didn't doubt for a moment what might happen.

And there was zilch he could do about it.

The waiter brought coffee. Topped Valentinian's mug. Smiled expectantly.

"Get him the hungry-spacer special," Valentinian said loud enough that Dave glanced at the menu in surprise. "Extra everything."

"Coming up."

Dave fell silent. Valentinian sipped freshly brewed coffee.

"That's it?" Dave whispered.

"Yeah," Valentinian blew out a heavy breath. "Don't tell me anything at this point, unless it helps keep us out of reach of whoever might want to ask questions about who you were before. I'm assuming we need to look at the possibility of running like hell. What are our odds?"

Dave watched him like a hawk. Studying. Again, re-calculating as the scales wavered back and forth.

"What about Madame Cleray?" Dave asked.

Valentinian shrugged again.

"I doubt she was involved," Valentinian offered. "Unless she was maneuvered into hiring me at the same time I was set up to need a first mate on Dominion Prime. There's always that."

Dave stiffened in such a way that Valentinian nearly threw his coffee in the man's face, as a prelude to seeing if he could make it to the door of the café fast enough to escape the assassin's reach.

"That would suggest an enormous conspiracy, just to kill the Dominator, wouldn't it?" Dave murmured quietly.

"Probably," Valentinian agreed. "And it still makes us all at least accomplices, even after the fact. The kind the new Dominator lines up against a wall and shoots, ya know?"

"Yeah, I do," Dave said. "I'm old enough to remember some of the aftermath when the last guy took power. You weren't even born yet. It got ugly for about a year, even though the former guy chose ritual suicide by triggering a new Tournament of Domination and then walking into the final battle and barely swinging his sword once. Lots of the old regime still had to be purged."

"And how bad do you suppose those purges might be this time, with the extra anger of an assassination layered on top of that like lemon frosting?" Valentinian questioned.

"Depends on the winner," Dave offered. "The Tournament won't start for another couple of months, because there has to be an open period for people to make their way to Cronus Prime and list their names. Then the Tournament itself takes about six weeks to complete. *Then* they form a new government and spread the good word across the Dominion. Maybe even start a new war, just as an excuse to give the new Dominator a chance to shine."

"You seem to know a lot about how this sort of thing works," Valentinian's voice wasn't accusing, but wasn't neutral either. Stark, perhaps.

"I had an…official capacity in the old Dominion," Dave admitted evasively. "My timing for departure is about as bad as my luck in finding you was good when I decided I wanted out."

It even sounded reasonable. Not that Valentinian figured it would keep him safe, but there wasn't anything he could do at this point but ride the main chance and offer prayers and whatever sacrifices he could to interested gods that might help.

Or plot a course for the far side of either Laurentia or Qetesh and abandon Madame Cleray and her girls here for the joys of Wildspace.

For the briefest moment, Valentinian even saw vulnerability in Dave's eyes. The kind that suggested the big man expected Valentinian to find the nearest White Hat and plead his case.

Except Valentinian already knew that his background would come up at that point, and they'd start digging. Hell, if Dave was honestly just fleeing from a bad marriage, Valentinian might spend more time in prison, if everything caught up with them.

Best not to find out.

"So we do nothing, say nothing," Valentinian said definitively. "Pretend like we're dumb spacers from the wrong side of the tracks and keep an eye out for people asking too many questions. I've already got a lifetime of experience at that sort of thing, so you're going to get to learn on the fly."

Dave looked like he wanted to argue, at least for a beat. Took a deep breath and marshalled his arguments for or against.

Thought better of it before he said something stupid and irrevocable.

Valentinian felt his own eyes go hard and cold. He was right back there in the Headmaster's office, desperately trying to deflect the avalanche coming down the mountainside at him, as he was chosen to be the ritual sacrifice, lest the other three boys get publically shamed.

One of these days, he would owe those fuckers a ration of pain. Maybe he'd sick Dave on them.

That brought a cold smile to Valentinian's face. Kind of matched the one on Dave's.

"Us against the galaxy, Vee?" Dave asked hesitantly.

"Something like that," Valentinian agreed. "You in?"

Dave stuck out his hand and Valentinian heard tumblers in a lock begin to fall into alignment.

"I'm in," the big man said.

They shook.

Us against the galaxy.

[13]
KYRIAKI

COMMERCIAL SPACE TRAVEL WAS WEIRD, Kyriaki decided. Previously, she had only ever flown on Security-owned ships, or as an honored passenger with the Dominion Armada.

Today she was pretending to be a civilian. It was something else she had never been, as her whole life had been originally aimed at joining the Solar Party and becoming a powerful bureaucrat. They were the ones that actually controlled the Dominion, no matter what the soldiers said.

Warriors were socialized to support the state, rather than a particular man or woman who held a position of authority.

We are all cogs in the greater Dominion.

Even being redirected into the White Hats of internal security hadn't really changed anything. She was still an aggressive climber. Now she stalked criminals, rather than deviationists, was all. The stalking was the same.

And the outcome was still a stronger Dominion.

Even if she had to laugh at the outrageous pun fortune had played on her. She was stalking a man on the thinnest of threads, because all other possible avenues had come up negative.

They were playing a longshot hypothesis. That maybe somehow Captain Tarasicodissa had managed to smuggle the assassin off the station, right under her very nose.

Longshot Hypothesis.

Now, she traveled as a civilian, 'little people' as she had always thought of them. It was turning into an eye-opening experience. Getting her papers checked regularly by hostile or bored bureaucrats who lacked adult supervision. Being told what to do and where to go, with no recourse. Ignored or verbally abused just because someone with authority could.

It rankled.

But it also marked her as being in a different class as an agent. No longer simply in burgundy and white, she could travel incognito and spy on the galaxy. It would make her reputation.

Or break it.

She would be able to report things about how the world worked when you weren't in power, and how things were being abused in such a way that it was wrong.

The things she saw left her with questions, and nobody to ask them to, at least until she got back to the Ambassador. Hopefully with Tarasicodissa's head in a vac-sealed bag, however a longshot that option might be.

That one was a traitor. She wasn't sure how or why she knew that, but the man was an enemy of the state. She would find his secret and expose him. And if he hadn't smuggled the assassin off Dominion Prime, he was still a criminal whose capture would make the Dominion a better place.

Longshot hypothesis or not.

Kyriaki had taken to retreating to her cabin after the common dinner, to brood in peace. The first night out, a man who worked in interplanetary sales and marketing had spent too much time attempting to solicit a sexual encounter between the two of them.

She considered it a victory that all she had done was turn him down and walk away, rather than throwing her drink in his face and then beating him to death. The thought had crossed her mind.

Random fornication with strangers was not her style.

But tonight, she had not retreated. Not slipped quietly away to hide from other humans in her cabin, watching the stars flow by at a rapid pace out her porthole.

Instead, she had found a small table with a good portal view and moved the other chair well away as an obvious invitation to not talk to her. A glass of hot chocolate lightly spiced with apple rum sat on the small table as she watched the endless night flow.

Kyriaki felt eyes upon her.

Not the fool salesman. He was clear across the room, trying his luck with some other desperate targets. She turned her head back to a table nearby. Not too close, but not that far away either.

He was older. Perhaps in his seventh or eighth decade. Slim almost to gauntness, like an arisen skeleton given flesh but not muscle. Thick, white hair wanted to frizz, but was kept buzzed short. Bright eyes almost golden matched her stare.

He lowered his gaze first, so as to not give offense.

When he looked up again, she was still watching him, so he smiled.

A gesture with his head asked an invitation to join her. Silently and politely.

Kyriaki wondered what a man her grand-sire's age might wish to discuss.

She was also intrigued. She nodded.

He rose like a snake stretching and easily lifted his chair

with one hand while holding a glass of dark wine in the other.

The man approached delicately and sat across from her in silence.

She felt his gaze, and his smile, but he turned pointedly to watch the night flowing by outside the portal.

After a moment, Kyriaki did the same, letting the silence stretch.

"It has been many years," the older man began in a low, strong voice. "I am an old man now, and long past my time. But I remember that walk."

She turned a sharp eye on the man.

"Discipline. Intention. Focus," he smiled at her. "One used to doing things with a strong hand, forced to refrain in public, while seeking something. Or someone. A hunter."

"And you were?" she asked, glancing around, but they were largely alone at this end of the lounge.

"Also a hunter, in my time," he nodded respectfully. "More than a seeker after wisdom, but it also includes seeking after truth. And masking your aura from those around you, as you approached."

Something about the way he spoke kept her from simply standing and walking away. For one, he had offered no offense, and spoken in a deliberately vague manner almost the opposite of that salesman over at the bar.

Respectful, and tactful. Something she had found missing on this journey, where she was just a young woman, apparently traveling alone.

Prey, perhaps, depending on the type of predator.

"And what did you stalk?" Kyriaki queried.

"The most dangerous quarries," he replied. "Men and women who sought to undermine the common good."

Kyriaki nodded. Something about the man had suggested a commonality to their pasts.

"What color?" she leaned forward to speak even more privately. It was a common phrase for suddenly-met strangers among the security organizations, with so many approaching similar problems from different angles.

"Gray initially," he also leaned close, like they were lovers sharing sweet words. "Burgundy, later."

And perhaps they were, at that.

"Indeed?" she smiled at him, warmer now than she had been.

Gray was the color of the Dominion's gendarmes, after they made it to the rank of detective. When they weren't hiding in plain clothes.

Burgundy was only worn by one force. The White Hats. Even pretending to be one in retirement was a crime that would merit time in a small, dank box.

She leaned back a little. Not enough to break the conversation, but to settle it on different ground.

"Kyriaki Apokapes," she introduced herself, nodding.

"Eridanos Argyros," he replied, smiling.

"And you are retired?" she asked.

"Forty-years of service was enough for me," he shrugged. "Especially as a widower with grown grandchildren. Now I travel some, visiting various elements of my extended family. And seek my own adventures, after a lifetime serving others. But you are just at the beginning of such a journey, no?"

"I am," she admitted.

"And in burgundy, unless I miss my guess," he whispered. "And hiding it well from the world."

"Yet you were able to notice?" Kyriaki asked, neither conceding nor denying.

"There is a way we walk," Eridanos grinned. "Men and women with righteousness on our side, and a secret power that no other in the Dominion possess. I could not describe it any other way, but to say I recognized myself when you walked across the room and sat."

"I see." Kyriaki wasn't sure if she should be pleased or annoyed. But at least she knew now to pay attention to her walk and display less pride.

"With the recent developments, is there a threat abroad?" he spoke quietly. "I have followed what news I could, removed from the seats of power by retirement."

Kyriaki felt her walls suddenly come back up. Possible former co-worker or not, the man was a stranger, at least until she could have someone track him down and vouch for his past.

And denying it would do her no good, if he was indeed a retired White Hat. Nor would it offend him. He would know how the process worked. At least well enough to follow.

She was in mufti, after all.

She settled for a shrug.

"I pursue a vague hint of a thread," she offered. "More senior officers are closer to the heart of the investigation."

Where they have found nothing in weeks of looking and talking to people.

"Then I wish you luck, Inspector," Eridanos said quietly. "I debark at Gui Xiu, but if I can be of any assistance, please do not hesitate to ask."

"Is your itinerary filed?" she asked.

"It was not," he admitted. "But I am an old man on my own time. I will correct that when I arrive. That way you can call upon me if we happen to cross paths later."

Kyriaki nodded. The ship did not have all the resources, but she would show her identcard to the right officials tomorrow and get all of the information they had on Eridanos Argyros. And then follow up if she needed, when she got to Tartarus.

LIANEARIA

AT LEAST THE two men had kept their polite distance up until now, both from the girls, as well as Lianearia's staff. Not that the adults were off-limits, if they chose not to be, but it spoke well for the two men that they had not risked the interpersonal friction that might come from anything more than a simple tumble.

Lianearia might be willing to stretch this charter as much as a year if things continued like this. Valentinian was charging less than Nash had, by more than a third, and yet the young man seemed happy with the deal.

Of course, he also wasn't attempting to maintain a significant organization of dead weight in the form of bouncers and hoodlums on various planets.

Lianearia approached the open door to the personal quarters on the first deck, not with trepidation, but perhaps concern, however poorly framed her guesses and instincts might be.

They had kept her alive and solvent for a very long time. She would listen to them.

She had been in this forward space only once, so she was

still getting used to a design that involved lowering the forward section of the deck by two steps for no reason she could identify except external aesthetics.

From the outside, it gave the forward section of the ship a shape almost like a bulldog hunched over a bone, with its tail a little elevated, at least when the cargo ramps were closed on the ground. Like now.

Lianearia could walk in utter silence, in any shoes. She had noticed that Dave Hall had the same skill, but that man was no dancer.

Still, she clicked her heels firmly on the steps as she approached. The room she was entering had been referred to as the rec room by both men, a space they would often retreat to after meals.

Valentinian was facing her as she entered, with Hall on her right, both seated as a small table that could come up out of the floor when needed.

"Right on time," Valentinian greeted her by standing and smiling, as did Hall. "Please, be seated."

She took the spot across from Hall and studied the two men. Their three weeks on Aestrolathia were among the most profitable, on a per-day scale, she had ever seen on this planet.

It helped that Nash wasn't around. Somehow, for all his friends and connections, his antics frequently caused her to have to pay more in bribes than budgeted.

She had always wondered if the man got a kickback from that. Now she was certain of it.

"We were just going over the itinerary for Tartarus," Valentinian began. "Dave's never been there, nor have I. What things should we know ahead of time?"

What, indeed?

Lianearia balanced the likely profitability of the upcoming section of the season, against having been nearly being stuck at Dominion Prime when the news erupted. Tartarus was where the money was best. She would have had to reschedule an entire month, or possibly skip Aestrolathia entirely, had they not been packed and gone as they had.

But that also meant that Nash had probably been stuck as well, trying to reorganize himself to deal with the *Longshot Hypothesis* crew, and then chase after Lianearia.

These two men had born out the good things her chandler had indicated, when she'd wanted to fire Nash. They needed to be prepared for that man's potential anger.

"I do not foresee changing the schedule of dates," she replied crisply to the young man. "However, it does mean that my former partner may make an appearance."

She noted the sly smile the two men shared. As though they had made the same connection.

"In the same circumstances, I would have headed directly to Tartarus as well," Valentinian said. "That would give him at least a week, even with the longer, commercial flight path, to prepare for whatever unpleasantness we are likely to encounter. How good are his friends?"

Lianearia stopped to consider that logic.

"He can be quite charming when necessary," she considered aloud. "As well as a punk when thwarted. I do not know what friends he might have, but I suspect that finances will be his issue. He was not prepared for me to terminate his contract and walk away, so he might be rather poor. And angry."

She liked the smile that played across Hall's face as she said that. Like the giant was looking forward to Nash's anger, in a personal way. Which just might make Nash even more desperate.

"Does he have any legal recourse?" Valentinian asked abruptly.

It was an astute question, especially from such a young

man. The Dominion was all about contract law. Courts could be merciless, but only about what was committed to paper.

"I have an exceptional lawyer on retainer," she grinned. "You saw how clean our contract is. There's power in not burying confusing details. Especially if you want the judge on your side later."

"Okay, so it will be personal," Valentinian nodded to Hall. "Bully boys doing stupid things because they think they can get away with it."

"How far do we let them push?" Hall asked in a dark, heavy voice that sent shivers down Lianearia's spine.

"Until we can get him in trouble with the authorities, and not us," Valentinian replied.

Lianearia was impressed. With both men. Neither were acting like innocents, here, but methodically planning a campaign to trap and potentially destroy her old partner, Axarnashalic 'Nash' Bogomelous. And do it for her.

White hands, and all that.

Lianearia could only imagine a future with that man not threatening her or her girls.

"So you do not plan to alter your published itinerary on Tartarus?" Valentinian focused his entire attention on her.

He seemed decades older when he did that, and not a bright boy just barely older than Defne or Nehir, the two oldest in the troupe.

"No," she growled fiercely. "I will not be put off by that man. If you two cannot thwart him, then perhaps I have chosen the wrong associates here."

It was a low blow, she knew. To challenge the manhood of the two men who had behaved themselves up until now. But she also didn't lean forward and bat her eyes at them either, like an ingénue in a melodrama.

Lianearia had prepared, just in case, wearing a top with a slash of a cut that would expose the inner lines of both breasts, if she leaned forward just right. Most men lost half their IQ points when she did that, but she was recruiting these men to perhaps do violence on her behalf, rather than seducing them.

This could be much more than a one-night engagement, if they were successful.

But she also knew that she had to approach the issue obliquely.

Neither man was what they seemed on first blush. Valentinian had a cruel streak that had come out a few times. Mostly in the words he chose, but also in the places he seemed to know from past experience. No innocent wanders accidentally into those sorts of locations.

And Hall…

She had not forgotten that night, watching him secretly as he walked through a dance with no partner but a sword and Death. Such skills were not widely taught, and she was sure the man was some sort of fugitive, perhaps even a renegade Caelon soldier.

Briefly, she had considered the possibility that Dave Hall might have been the assassin that ended a Dominator's life. At the time she had hired Valentinian, she had noted a first mate, but apparently that man had left, and Hall had joined the crew from the Dominion Prime station.

He did not feel like an assassin, however. Too much of the man was only one layer deep. A good social killer must first be like a good courtesan, able to bury everything so deep as to disappear into a role. Dave Hall was a soldier. Nothing more.

But even that was more than Nash would be able to recruit, especially if his finances had fallen on hard times. That man would scrape the docks and bars for bouncers and buffoons. It might take a dozen to threaten Dave Hall effectively, especially if he was holding that sword at the time. And that didn't take into account her or Valentinian.

The captain might be wearing a pistol at all times, but Lianearia had both a pocket stunner and a short blade with her constantly these days.

The conversation had fallen to silence. She supposed that was her fault. She had simply left the two men speechless. And hadn't even had to use sex to do it.

Pity, she supposed. Either man looked like he might be fun in bed, in the right circumstances.

These were not those.

"So I will presume that you have the outer ring of security taken care of?" she asked in a sweet, almost-innocent voice.

"The outer ring?" Valentinian challenged.

"If I have to, I will shoot Nash myself," she announced. "Hopefully, it won't come to that."

[15]

DAVE

FROM ORBIT, Dave didn't think Tartarus looked all that impressive. A little more blue than most planets he had known, at least seen from this altitude. A little less brown. The usual number of orbital stations, diamonds in the darkness of the night matching the wide swathes of lights on the night side below.

Dave leaned forward just a little to watch the planet below.

He found it intriguing that Madame Cleray's arc of planets she toured generally remained away from the bigger, wealthier ones. She was playing what they might charitably call the second tier of Dominion worlds. The places without as significant a home-grown entertainment industry. Or a different kind perhaps, geared more towards sporting events and such, and less into the sorts of impressive singing and choreographic expertise of Solaria Femina.

Playing the small-town venues, as it were, rather than the bright lights, where she had to compete with the megastars that had entire touring caravans.

No, the woman and her troupe could make more money

here, especially with what she was paying Valentinian. But the captain owned the ship outright, so he didn't need to make regular payments to bankers, like most others did in this industry.

And Valentinian could haul cargo and passengers in equal amounts, if he needed to, specializing in speed between planets when something needed to be there quickly.

That was one of the reasons Dave had picked *Longshot Hypothesis* to make his escape. That and a captain with a shadowy past and a well-developed paranoia that would keep him away from immediately assisting the authorities, if something came up.

The White Hats would focus all their efforts on Valentinian, hopefully, ignoring the big, hulking brute known to the galaxy as Dave Hall.

At least until he found a safe, quiet way to get entirely outside of the Dominion and never look back. It had to be quiet, because the Dominion's borders would not stop that kind of retribution. It would barely delay it.

Dave would still need to maintain a low profile out there, unless he wanted to go all the way to Wildspace and try his luck. The thought had crossed his mind, more than once.

"Ground Control, this is *Longshot Hypothesis*," Valentinian called out from his captain's chair. "Maintaining de-orbital path on schedule. This will be our final check in until we get below atmospheric ionization."

"Acknowledged, *Longshot Hypothesis*," the reply came crisply as Dave listened. "Skies are clear on your path at present. Keep eyes down for unregistered country vessels, as they do not file a flight plan unless they will be making a sustained high orbit."

"Roger that."

Dave watched the young man move with expert grace, toggling switches and adjusting dials minutely as the big ship began to flare down into the thicker air below them. The ship flew like a hawk under his guidance.

Dave could see the time spent at Gymnasia Dominia in the motions. While it was a pity Valentinian would never join the Armada, that was in turn a good thing for Dave, as this level of piloting expertise in a budding, young pirate was rare.

"You ready to take control?" Valentinian asked with a sly smile.

Dave took a deep breath and contemplated all the controls. It was much more than stepping into the arena to duel, because here everything became your enemy, but this was much more predictable.

And Dave had been spending time flying simulated take-offs and landings, just so he could eventually do something like this. Maybe even buy his own ship, one of these days, if he could get as good a deal as the reports said Valentinian had.

But then, when Anuradha finally fell four years ago, their entire government-owned merchant fleet fell with it, so cargo transports had gotten cheap. Everybody who wanted to had immediately upgraded, a process that rippled across the entire Dominion economy.

And allowed people like Valentinian Tarasicodissa to buy his own ship. And eventually hire a guy named Dave Hall as his first mate.

"Taking control," Dave said carefully as he reached out and just rested his fingertips on the right buttons.

Valentinian grinned and leaned back in his chair to watch. That was a ruse, Dave was sure. At the first sign of trouble, Valentinian would override and lock him out.

As he should.

Still, no time like the present.

Dave pressed the first button and control flowed to his

board. Altitude: just so. Pitch currently starting to nose down, so they could slice into the thickening air like a sword in an overhead strike. Later, he would flare the nose back and force a glide as a way to bleed off speed. The lateral cut. That would be when he had to watch the boards for too much heat.

All systems green.

"Initiating," Dave announced in a low voice.

Outside, the horizon suddenly leaned up into the air, relative to the dashboard. Dave added a little thrust, and *Longshot Hypothesis* began to fall out of the sky.

Hopefully, only metaphorically.

[16]

NASH

Nash watched the morning sky, as if the Creator would send him a lightning bolt as a sign of favor.

Or something like that.

The view out the office's window was spectacular, facing north as the sun was a third of the way across the path in front of him.

He needed a little luck right now. That bitch Cleray had picked the worst possible moment to dump him in the gutter, and only old favors had gotten him this far and kept him out of jail.

Friends had scored him a ticket onto the liner to Tartarus ahead of Lianearia and her girls. Other contacts had found him some office space to spoof, while he leaned on an old lawyer friend to draw up some new contracts giving him shares of the corporation that would end up owning Solaria Femina when this was all done. Three of them, ranging from complete control, to fifty-one percent, to twenty-five percent.

That had been his mistake before, letting her retain control of the girls while he handled all the booking and travel. It had let that bitch cut him out when he wasn't looking.

Now there would be better contracts. Even partial ownership that would mean she couldn't just get rid of him. The woman just needed to understand that she'd be nothing without all his friends and contacts, and that he needed to be rewarded commensurately.

And if she didn't agree, well then maybe things would have to get a little rough.

Nash was more than willing to start at twenty-five percent. That was enough cash to set him up for his other gigs and swindles. Creator only knew how much money Lianearia Cleray had cost him, by pulling the rug out from under him on Dominion Prime, just as he was arranging for some personal performances by the girls for some very high-ranking men in the Solar Party.

Secretly, of course. Cleray would have blown a gasket if she found out. The girls were always marketed with a heavy layer of virginal innocence, but even Nash knew the truth about that.

Sümeyye Daimonoioannes, the Chastitymaster, existed to protect the girls from random fans, not to maintain their complete and utter innocence from all things worldly.

As far as he knew, only half of them were probably still virgins, and that was just because those few had some silly notion that it would increase their resale value on the market later, when they couldn't be in the group anymore.

Plus the one with the religious restriction against being impure outside of the sanctity of marriage.

Whatever.

All he needed was a solid voice in the boardroom. Or to at least to force Cleray to move from a sole proprietorship to something more easy to manipulate.

Oh, the joys of corporate law.

A phone rang on the desk. He checked the name displayed. A local fixer who owed him several favors.

"Good news?" Nash asked Arturious.

"Maybe, boss," the man replied. "Solaria Femina is on pretty good terms with the guy here in town, but he owes some people some favors that we might be able to push forward until he owes you instead."

"Push," Nash decided. "Find out what it is that we can call on, in the way of resources. If we have to be sneaky, then that needs to be on the table at the top. I don't want a repeat of what happened to us on Dominion Prime, okay?"

"Was he really that good, the guy you ran into?" Arturious's voice sounded skeptical.

"There were five guys, pal," Nash sneered. "He took them all. And that wasn't the sort of place where I could just whip out a pistol and shoot the son of a bitch, you know?"

"Got it," the ex-bouncer with the nasally voice from a previously-broken nose replied. "Fewer gendarmes around here, and enough of them can be paid to look the other way."

"Get me prices, Arturious," Nash growled, letting his anger color the tones. "Favors owed, cash we can collect on, favors we can push. Cleray's nothing without her new bouncer and I intend to make sure of that."

"Sure thing, boss."

The line went dead.

Nash snarled to himself as he slammed the receiver down. No, Cleray was just a dame he could push around, if she didn't have Valentinian Tarasicodissa handy.

Nash had looked the kid up, afterwards. There hadn't been much else he could do, with the station on hard lockdown before he could score a ship to go after the *Longshot Hypothesis.*

The kid was a player, that much was obvious. Hadn't spent much time on Cronus Prime or Dominion Prime, or

Nash probably would have met him at some point. Dangerous, but only to a certain degree. Former Dominion golden boy gone rogue.

But he was just one man. And without Valentinian around, Nash had no worries about the big bruiser. Couple of quick jolts from a shock pistol and that guy would be hamburger.

Nash smiled.

Revenge was going to be ice cream.

[17]

KYRIAKI

Tartarus. Almost as remote a backwater as Aestrolathia would have been, had Kyriaki chased them to their first stop after the escape.

This planet was probably worse, if she had to rank them, based purely on their industrial might. Aestrolathia was largely an agrarian culture, so large swaths of the planet were given over to raising animals and growing grains, while Tartarus was a center for heavy industry.

Walking out of the starport and looking for a taxi, Kyriaki could taste the grit and ozone in the air. She supposed that she had been spoiled by the pure air of living on a space station, especially one like Dominion Prime, but she couldn't imagine people wanting to live like this.

Ergo, most of them probably didn't, and this place was a trap that people would escape, any chance they had. Or seek their escapism in frivolous things, like concerts by touring musical groups. It made a queer sort of sense, then, why Solaria Femina would come here.

Larger acts could play extended residencies on resort

worlds. Or just tour the big places, like Cronus Prime. A hustler like Lianearia Cleray would have to work the corners.

Lucky for Kyriaki, Cleray had hired an even worse hustler in Valentinian Tarasicodissa. Corrupt, ugly planets like Tartarus would be their playground. And their downfall.

Kyriaki had considered approaching the local internal security apparatus, but she had her doubts as to the brilliance of such a move. Briefing notes from the Ambassador looked to be intentionally vague on the topic but suggested that even the White Hats here had leaks. If she showed up and filed a report, it would probably make its way to Tarasicodissa quickly enough.

Creator only knew if the man would flee, knowing that she was closing in on him. Or where he might go. While that might be the sort of admission of guilt she could use to request a task force, the same level of escalation that resulted would take the investigation right back out of her hands, handing control off to a local Ambassador, or at least senior Inquisitors.

And she wanted that man herself.

So Kyriaki skipped traveling to the local Palace of Law. She had that option, as long as she considered the risks too high. Or whatever excuse she could make stick so she didn't give her prey any warning she was coming.

And she hadn't lost her chops at working the streets for information, just because she had been working at the center of the universe. First stop, the theater where they would be playing in three days, just to scout the neighborhood around it and determine the best way to approach Lianearia Cleray.

Nothing had ever managed to stick to the woman, in spite of her time in the vicinity of her former partner, the infamous *Nash* Bogomelous that Kyriaki had read so much about on the flight out here. That one should have been arrested at Dominion Prime. By the time everything was sorted out, he had vanished as well.

Kyriaki pulled her jacket a little tighter around herself, slid a hand inside to just touch the stun pistol she wore, and set off to learn this new city.

VALENTINIAN CHECKED the charge on his shock pistol, out of habit, as he and Dave emerged from the forward airlock into the late afternoon sun. And gloom.

Tartarus stank. Too much industrial effluvium cast into the sky to fall as acid rain somewhere else. It etched metal surfaces rough anywhere it landed, and bled paints quickly.

Depending on how long they stayed in places like this, he might have to consider spending a week in a dry basin, or a desert world like Amenhotep, and refinish the outer hull. That would be good practice for Dave to learn the exterior maintenance.

Valentinian smiled as he considered how he might convince Madame Cleray to join him under a solar umbrella nearby on a hill, watching Dave and the dancers work, stripped down as far as necessary in the heat and sun.

"What's so funny?" Dave asked from his right as they set off across the tarmac to the main terminal. Unlike Solaria Femina, he and Dave walked the kilometer, as long as it wasn't raining. The girls rode in local taxi buses. As would he, when the air got bad enough.

He had gotten lucky today. Forecast was for the unsafe rain to hold off until tomorrow.

"Maintenance never ends," Valentinian said obliquely.

Nine dancers. Five or six adult women that might not look too bad in bikinis, or completely topless, depending on the planet they might have originally been born on and their willingness to eliminate tan lines.

"Whatever," Dave rumbled. "Plan?"

"Madame Cleray put us on the guest list tonight with backstage passes," Valentinian replied with a bigger grin as they walked. "We're going to go into town, get some food, and then go to a show."

"Ship safe while we're gone?" Dave glanced back.

Valentinian had locked the ship, and also locked all the interior bulkheads as well. Solaria Femina was staying in town this week, since they had performances in three different venues.

And everybody wanted some space, after nearly six weeks cooped up.

"I'm not sure *you* could get in," Valentinian replied. "And I warned the port police that there might be an attempt at sabotage. Even corrupt bastards like those don't want a reputation for letting bad shit happen on their watch."

"Sabotage?" Dave's eyes got big.

"Our buddy Nash might stick to juvenile delinquency," Valentinian grinned. "And he might not. If I thought he would actually try something here, one of us would be hiding nearby with a pain rifle."

"Ouch," Dave shrugged and turned back to match Valentinian's pace. "What about the bar? Anything likely to happen there?"

"Doubt it," Valentinian said. "Too many witnesses in a public place. Plus too much they won't know about either of us. If I were him, I'd hire someone we don't know to keep watch on us and find a spot they might ambush us later. That's sort of thing I'm still expecting. Tartarus is that kind of planet. That's why I'm walking around with the strap off my holster and the safety off."

"You don't fool around, do you?"

"I don't like bullies, Dave," Valentinian groused. "People with power abusing it on people that can't stop them. That's probably my one and only button. If the rules were evenly applied, I'd either be an Armada officer right now, or those other three bastards would have gone down with me. If Nash wants to play rough, I'll teach him a few things even you probably don't know."

"I've seen some jagged and ugly things, Vee," Dave replied. "Done some, too."

"Probably." Valentinian felt his stride stretching as his anger worked its way into his legs. "But did you ever get vindictively crude on someone, after you had knocked them down, just to win the next fight?"

"The next fight?" Dave asked as he kept up.

"Curb stomp someone after you've beaten them, Dave," Valentinian felt his mind go back to that place. "Not just break an arm or a leg, but kill them, so that you get a reputation for savagery so out of size with your normal character that nobody messes with you after that?"

"No," Dave was quiet. "In the arena, there are iron rules for behavior. On the battlefield, it is always about efficiency. Put your target down with shots to center mass and move on as soon as they stop being an active threat."

"Exactly my point," Valentinian said. "Nash doesn't know me, most likely, or discounts what others might have seen or said. If he shows up, it will be necessary to educate the man."

Valentinian noted the scowl on Dave's face, but he fell silent.

Those were ugly memories. Valentinian was a little taller

than average for a guy. Lanky and good looking in the way that women liked. But he wasn't a fighter like Dave. He'd rather fast talk his way out of trouble than shoot, given the option.

Sometimes that wasn't an option.

And having Dave handy had been sheerest luck.

He hadn't expected to see Nash on Aestrolathia. That place was too polite and well-mannered for the most part.

Tartarus was the sort of place that spawned people like Nash.

Somehow, he knew he'd see that bastard eventually.

TARTARUS WAS ALWAYS one of her favorite places to bring Solaria Femina. Lianearia could always count on sold-out shows and a surge in record sales when they came here. Didn't matter if they stayed just in Tartarus City for a full week, the girls wouldn't wear out their welcome.

And then, depending, maybe a quick tour of some of the secondary cities. Or perhaps a chat with some of her old contacts about playing special shows directly at some of the bigger factories. Always a good way to provide the bosses a good tax break for hosting 'team-building entertainment' while still charging employees a good fee.

Everybody came out ahead.

And so far, no hints, not even a whisper, that suggested Nash was anywhere on the planet. Hopefully, that sorry son of a bitch had finally pushed his luck one iota too far. Or crossed the wrong people when his pockets were empty.

She would enjoy a future without having to look over her shoulder for that bastard.

As the bus pulled to the rear of the theater, Lianearia was out first and carefully counting noses as everyone followed.

For this first performance, she had brought everyone from the hotel, rather than just the field team. Best to keep it organized. They could always loosen things up tomorrow night.

The air was heavy tonight. About normal for fall on Tartarus, this far south, inland just far enough that the ocean breezes had a hard time pushing the exhaust from smoke stacks over the nearby mountain range.

The forecast was heavier weather tomorrow night, but that was the weekend, so the crowds would still be heavy, but tonight might be like a Friday night, if people decided to get out tonight, and stay in tomorrow.

Either way, the money taken at the front door should be a lovely amount. Especially if she didn't have Nash slipping his greedy fingers in and perhaps letting some of it vanish by the time it got to her.

The rear door was open as the girls all filed inside, with her at the end of the column. Kostantina and Fahrettin had them lined up when she caught up.

"Darling, so good to see you," the manager greeted her with air kisses on both sides.

Tahllin had owned this place for decades, a fixture on the entertainment circuit, a beaming little gnome of a man, completely bald and utterly irrepressible. But entirely homosexual, and not the least bit of a threat to anyone, except perhaps Fahrettin.

As if anyone might be a danger to top her Songmaster, perhaps the greatest threat to decorum that Lianearia knew.

"Any surprises?" Lianearia asked breezily, hoping deep inside that nothing had changed except the fashion horses working the front of the stage.

"Nothing is allowed to be a surprise, at my age," Tahllin beamed at her. "Not even this year's crop of pretty boys."

"As it should be, Tahllin," Lianearia kissed the man again, right atop his bald pate.

She turned by stepping to the gnome's side and surveyed her corps of troops in two lines, drawn up with the sort of military precision that Kostantina brought to the table.

She clapped twice, just for effect, as everyone was already paying attention.

"To your rooms for makeup and costuming," she ordered peremptorily.

The group even pivoted and walked in harmonious unity as she watched, alert to every detail.

"And now?" Tahllin asked as they were suddenly alone.

"A glass of wine for me and an hour for them to begin to get organized," Lianearia replied. "My new transport captain and his first mate will probably join us after that, and then the show is still expected in ninety minutes?"

"Anybody but you, my dear, and I would expect them to eventually saunter out sulkily in perhaps two hours," Tahllin's smile broadened. "Hopefully the locals remember to be prompt."

"Indeed," Lianearia smiled. "I have two new songs that will be debuted tonight, at the top of each set. Never before heard in public. Brand new choreography. Everything. Just for you, Tahllin."

"Oh, how you do spoil me," he said. "The bartenders know you, so I will leave you to your adventures. Try not to seduce too many of them away from me. I've only just now gotten them broken in to my tastes and if you spoil them, I will never forgive you."

He departed and left her alone in the back area that combined a warehouse feel with a loading dock. Through the walls to the front, she could hear the thumping beat of the latest dance tunes that were just now starting to peak on

Tartarus, running, as usual, somewhere around eight weeks behind the capital.

But there was no accounting for taste. And even warpships required some element of lag to get from here to there, so the tastemakers of Cronus Prime would always be out at the forefront, if for no other reason than they could.

What was the use in being the center of the universe, if you didn't make everyone else adapt their music and fashions to you?

Lianearia smiled secretly to herself as she emerged from the door with "Staff Only" on the other side.

Out here, the noise was a solid thing. Dense enough, with the artificial smoke, to be almost painful. It certainly accentuated the feel of the dirty air outside, even though she knew just how hard the blowers on the roof were working to filter the air.

She approached the bar with the judicious use of hips and elbows, probably leaving a few of these pretty children with bruises they would see for a week.

That's what you get for being in my way, youngsters. Toughen up if you want to play in the big leagues.

About half of the bartenders were new from when she'd been here last year. And Tahllin had obviously briefed the old-timers that she would be coming. It took a look and a quick gesture for one of them to hand her a glass of the good wine, the stuff that came from the bottom shelf under the bar, rather than the refilled bottles on the backbar.

Good, red wine. Made from real grapes, rather than grape juice and industrial alcohol.

She swirled it in her glass as she surveyed the room. Already halfway full, and they still had more than an hour until showtime. With more people lined up at the door for the bouncers to admit.

It would be good.

Would have been good.

A woman emerged from the crowd with that look in her eyes. The kind that had a purpose in approaching, rather than a fan looking for an introduction or an autograph.

She looked to be in her mid-twenties, so more than a decade younger than Lianearia, but there was a hard edge to the girl that most women don't learn until they're looking backwards at thirty, itself rapidly receding in the mirror.

While this stranger was dress casually, Lianearia wasn't in the least bit fooled. She wore it wrong, and Lianearia was an expert on how to use fashion as a weapon.

Beige slacks a little too baggy to show off obviously strong thighs and hips. A tucked-in shirt in a cotton probably chosen more for comfort than fit, as the girl didn't have the beginnings of a spare tire that many developed when their metabolism slowed faster than their habits.

You can never outrun the fork in your hand.

Black jacket that was the opposite of every other woman in the room, as it aimed for quiet and obscure, when the children in here were trying to impress men and find themselves a Prince Charming to take them away from the drudgery of line work in a factory.

It almost made the girl look like a cop. Except her brown hair was pulled up and to one side in a bun that looked like it wanted to be under a hat.

"Lianearia Cleray?" the stranger asked in a voice that sounded forced, as if being polite wasn't her default position.

"That's right," Lianearia replied, sipping at her wine and trying to determine why a cop would be working the inside of Tahllin's club. They knew better than that. The man paid off the right people not to have his guests accosted. The bouncers would simply toss you outside in handcuffs for the gendarmes outside to arrest, if you got out of hand.

And they would get their handcuffs back afterwards. Of

course, bright pink shimmering manacles, emblazoned with TAHLLIN'S in gold could only be found in one place.

You could even get your own pair in the gift shop, if you were into that sort of thing.

The woman reached inside her jacket and pulled out a card-reader that she held close to her stomach as she opened. She displayed a badge that made Lianearia's blood go cold.

"Dominion Security," the woman said simply. "I'd like to ask you a few questions. Is there someplace private we can talk?"

That explained the hair, if nothing else. She was used to wearing it under a beret.

White Hats.

What the hell had Nash done now?

Or worse, Tarasicodissa?

[20]
KYRIAKI

WHEN IN DOUBT, spook your target. It was a lesson Kyriaki had learned early. Frightened people make mistakes, which you can use against them later.

Cleray hadn't remembered her face, but Kyriaki wasn't surprised. It had been a simple-enough customs inspection, back on Dominion Prime.

Nobody outside the Household had even known that the Dominator was dead at that point. She had been professional, and mostly focused on Captain Tarasicodissa anyway. Lianearia Cleray had been almost an afterthought.

She followed the woman back through a door marked "Staff Only" into a quieter part of the building, and then into an empty office. Cleray sat behind the desk, like perhaps it was her office, but Kyriaki wasn't in the mood to cede a centimeter to the woman. Instead, she kipped a hip up onto the side of the desk and rested her weight as she closed the door to give them whatever semblance of privacy they might have.

It had the extra advantage of letting her look down on

the taller woman. Cleray hadn't been expecting that, from the ugly glare in her eyes.

"What can I help the White Hats with?" Cleray scowled. "I am a law-abiding citizen in good standing."

Like that would help, if I really wanted to grieve you, lady.

But Kyriaki didn't say that out loud. It was even the honest truth. Nothing had come up, regardless of the amount of digging Kyriaki had done. Nor the direction.

Only her various accomplices had ever been wanted or arrested.

So far.

"We're investigating Captain Tarasicodissa," Kyriaki said simply. "As you are currently chartering his vessel, I wanted to know if you had seen or heard anything of interest to Dominion Security. Yours was one of the last vessels to depart from Dominion Prime before the news came out that the Dominator had been assassinated."

"And you think Tarasicodissa had something to do with it?" Cleray let her amusement show.

Or she was a good actress, as well as a dancer, songwriter, and businesswoman.

"We're following up on a number of possible threads," Kyriaki let her voice trail off, like this was just the first and least interesting thing about the investigation, instead of the entirety of it, as far as her bosses were probably concerned.

She could always bring in help, if she felt the situation warranted it. And would immediately lose control, but would hopefully get a gold star next to her name, if something did come out of it later.

"Well, at present, the man has hauled my troupe from Dominion Prime to Aestrolathia to here," Cleray scoffed. "And in that time, neither him nor his first mate have even made a pass at myself or one of my girls. If he's smuggling anything, you should take it up with the customs inspectors who had failed at their job, because all of the gear in that cargo bay belongs to me, except for one junk box in a corner where they throw broken pieces they haven't gotten around to fixing."

"I see." Kyriaki supposed she did.

The man's swindles weren't likely to be as brazen as Cleray's former partner. And Kyriaki herself had signed off on the customs inspection at Dominion Prime, but that had been barely more than a walking tour of the ship.

By now, it would be too late to find anyone that Tarasicodissa might have smuggled out in a hidden compartment. The best she could do would be to have the ship impounded and then bring in a team of experts to gut it, looking. But she didn't have enough of anything at this point to get a judge to sign that kind of warrant.

And Cleray probably knew that. The woman's contracts on file on Dominion Prime showed a much higher level of legal expertise than most former dancers should have had.

"What I would prefer at this point is that you keep your eyes open," Kyriaki said. "Without mentioning me to Tarasicodissa or anyone else, lest you become an accomplice and we have to bring you in to sweat you."

That registered a hit.

Nobody wants to be arrested by the White Hats. It was a useful psychological edge.

"Well, if you wish to talk to the man, he is supposed to be here tonight," Cleray tried to sound tough, but her eyes showed the slightest trace of fear now. "Will that be all?"

"It will," Kyriaki smiled. "We prefer the willing assistance of Dominion citizens in our investigations."

She pulled a card from her inside pocket, just touching her pistol with her knuckles as a kind of good luck totem as she did. No way she was chirping a total stranger's machine. Especially not a potential suspect.

"This has my local contact information, should you need to reach me," Kyriaki said.

"Kyriaki Apokapes?" Cleray confirmed.

"That's right, Madame Cleray," Kyriaki let her smile turn a little more hostile. "I'm staying here in Tartarus City for now."

Kyriaki rose and opened the door, making her way out of the back of the club and to the front. She would take up a quiet corner, away from the dancers competing for attention down front, and see what came up.

[21]

NASH

TAHLLIN'S HADN'T CHANGED one bit. Nash didn't recognize the three bouncers protecting the front door, but that was nothing new. Those boys came and went with regularity. None of them would know him, either.

Once inside, Nash made his way carefully, watching the crowd slowly growing. The mob was large enough already to give him anonymity. And Tahllin had called to let him know that Lianearia had arrived. She would be in back initially, supervising things, until she came up front for the one glass of wine she allowed herself at the beginning of the evening.

There.

He watched her emerge from the back. Make her way to the bar, still as beautiful and dominant as she had been since she stopped singing at the front of the group. Nash had watched old videos from the early days. It was amazing what she had accomplished since then with his help.

Now she just needed to recognize that she would be nothing without him. However that had to happen.

He considered confronting her now, but the timing wasn't right. His hired hands wouldn't be ready, so he hovered near a pillar and watched, obscured by shadows, lights, and bodies.

It gave him a thrill, to consider her begging him to come back into her life. Giving him a permanent slice of the pie, so he could work on making things really big, and not just playing second-rate planets all over the Dominion.

Lianearia really had no idea what sort of power and possibility she was sitting on here. Again, he was just the man to educate her.

A woman approached Lianearia, as he watched. Spoke with her briefly.

Nash watched the nods and body language. This seemed important.

Lianearia turned and walked into the back. The stranger followed, glancing once around the room to make sure she wasn't followed.

Interesting.

Has dear Lianearia tired of her pretty boy already? Was he inadequate to her needs, that she was already shopping around for her next victim?

The stranger was a woman, but far too old to be a potential dancer joining the group. No, she had a more official look, as if she represented some greater organization.

Was Lianearia about to take the step into the big time without him? That would never do.

Not the upgrade. That was already in the cards. But he would need to be cut in on that deal ahead of time, whatever it was. Especially if it meant slicing off the new captain who had caused Nash such troubles at Dominion Prime. Lianearia had caught him at a moment when all their various contracts were closed off, just before they were to sign the new ones.

How better to insert himself again, than at that very instant when Lianearia was already about to open a new chapter?

Nash controlled himself before he preened. It took everything he had not to dance a little jig as he considered the future rolling out in front of him.

Let Lianearia get rid of her little transport captain boy, and be all set to hire a new one, and he could just swoop in and take charge of everything, like he was meant to.

It would be so lovely, finally getting that woman to understand the natural way of things.

He watched the two women disappear into the back and thought happy thoughts as the crowd slowly built around him, jostling him occasionally but still not harming the happiness that seemed to flow off his being. A few females passing close even smiled at him, sensing the joy he exuded, even if they were completely clueless as to the origin.

In other circumstances, he might even chat a few of them up, but he had too many other things to accomplish tonight. Perhaps tomorrow he would be in a position to seduce one of these lovely, foolish young ladies into doing things she would be embarrassed to admit later to her rabbi.

For now, he settled in to watch.

As DIVES AND DANCEHALLS WENT, Valentinian did think the joint wasn't all that impressive. Three dumb bouncers at the front. Two of the men looked like what everyone expected bouncers to be like. Nearly as tall as Dave, but much heavier, with bulk making up for the lethality his first mate brought to the table.

The third one was the dangerous-looking one, at least to Valentinian. Shorter than Valentinian and skinny. Wiry in ways that suggested he would be a mongoose to the other two men's sluggish bears.

Not that Valentinian was planning to start trouble here tonight, but you never knew on a strange planet.

He had moved his shock pistol to a shoulder holster under his jacket back on the ship. Here, it just got an eyebrow raised, but nothing more. Which told Valentinian what kind of joint this was.

Not that he had any doubts. Tartarus City had a reputation as a hard place. Carrying a shock pistol wasn't illegal, nor would a stunner be. Only something heavier would cause the bouncers to refuse entry.

Which just meant that they had superior firepower on call, if they thought they needed it. That thought actually brought greater peace to Valentinian, although Dave remained twitchy. Not enough bar fights in his time, obviously.

They ended up at the bar first, where they got translucent, plastic cups of thin, watery beer that still cost too many Solars. Again, Valentinian wasn't really surprised. Places like this made their money at the bar, not the front door.

Water down the drinks and add some salt as well to make you thirsty. Free salty snacks. Play the music loud and energetic, to get you dancing and sweaty, so you needed to buy more. It was a scam, but a legitimate-enough one.

Valentinian just knew he was just too cheap to hang out at places like this for fun. He preferred the quiet dives where the drinks were honest and the pretty people elsewhere.

He led Dave to a side wall and found a booth up on a head-high, elevated walkway over the room, with a good view of the dance floor and the stage. He had seen Solaria Femina practicing their routines in the cargo bay, but never with all the right lighting and sound gear. To say nothing of the costumes he expected.

It would be a fun night, assuming no trouble. And even Nash wouldn't be stupid enough to show up the first night and start trouble. He'd need time to scout the ground. Heading home later, maybe. More likely tomorrow.

"So we just sit here?" Dave ask/yelled over the thumping earthquake of the song playing.

"I am," Valentinian called back. "Feel free to go down and dance, or drink some more. I'm only buying the first round."

Dave grinned at him and sat back, looking like a just-fed lion surrounded by hyenas and rabbits. Valentinian wondered where that put him, but not too much. If Dave wanted to get laid, he knew the way back to the ship, and the codes to open the airlock.

Hopefully, the man would have the sense to get a room in town, rather than bring a date back to the ship, but they'd burn that bridge if it became necessary. Dave had been good crew, so far, so Valentinian wouldn't begrudge the man blowing off some steam.

He just didn't want to deal with the bimbos on the dance floor. And he was too cheap to find a professional. At least tonight. Give him another month or three surrounded by all those gorgeous teenagers and he might be chasing after the cook, Hiranur. She was the nicest to be around of all of them anyway.

Valentinian felt old. And Dave struck him as a rookie. It was a weird reversal of the normal flow of things. Especially since Dave had kids his age.

But he supposed it was the light-years, and not the seasons that counted. Dave had apparently been pretty sheltered for a long time, which didn't surprise Valentinian. The Caelons were an insular group, and Valentinian had no doubt the man had been one of the Dominator's Assault Cavalry troopers. No other branch had that way of walking, proud and arrogant in their utter disdain for little people.

Not that Dave had ever pulled that shit, but it was in the eyes. The set of the shoulders. Even the way the man walked.

Killer.

Even the girls around here picked up on it, going out of their way to walk by and smile at the big man. Valentinian was used to being the center of attention with lots of pretty girls, and he got his share of looks, but they had a hunger in their eyes when they looked at Dave.

Valentinian shrugged and decided that he might be getting in Dave's way. Chasing off the girls who might be of a mind to just walk up and slide into the booth to breathlessly introduce themselves. It had happened to Valentinian more than once.

Dave would probably be shocked out of his mind the first time some girl did it to him. Valentinian slid to the edge of the booth with a grin.

The big guy needed a little R&R.

"What's up?" Dave called.

"Nothing," Valentinian replied. "Just going to scout the joint and hit the head before there's a line. Maybe find Madame Cleray and say hello."

"I'll come with you," Dave suddenly looked uncomfortable and started to join him.

"You stay here," Valentinian waved him back. "Save the table and keep an eye on the crowd. And don't let too many pretty girls seduce you."

He liked the way Dave's face blushed. The man probably had no clue how badly he might carbonate the hormones of some of these women. Impregnate them just by smiling their way with that lion face of his.

Valentinian laughed to himself and aimed for the front of the building, next to the main bar off to the side of the stage. Take a leak first and then go find their employer.

At least tonight would give him some time to relax.

[23]
NASH

Oh, my, what have we here?

Nash hadn't seen Captain Tarasicodissa enter the club, but there he was. Walking along towards the bar with apparently no care in the world. And he had missed Nash in the crowd, but that was as much by luck as by design.

Tonight, Nash had gone in for black and gray. It would stand out only if he decided he wanted to get out on the dance floor with some pretty filly, since they were all in the brightest outfits imaginable. Colors across the entire spectrum, bound together only by being tight and metallic and occasionally sheer, if you saw them turn the right way.

Advertising sexual promiscuity in the loudest, and yet most subtle way possible.

Perhaps another time. Not only was Lianearia Cleray here, but so was her doxie, Tarasicodissa.

My, my, my. What fun can we have with this?

Nash moved in along a parallel course to the man. The club was enormous, but there were only so many places you could go inside. He followed the young captain down past the bar and watched him enter the restroom.

That was too compact a space. Nash would probably be noticed. Might even just run into the man coming as the youngster was going, and possibly be recognized.

No, that would just never do.

Surely Lianearia had warned the boy that things weren't over between them, hadn't she?

Instead of following, Nash pulled out his card-reader and sent a quick message off to Arturious, patiently waiting with a few friends in a large land truck a few blocks away. Letting him know there would be two guests for dinner, rather than one. Nothing incriminating enough to be used against them later, as it were.

He found a spot and waited. If the youngster was here, it was possible his overly-dangerous crewman was as well.

There. Seated on the sidewall, surrounded at a discreet distance by young women like a pack of wolves seeking to bring down an ox. Just so, they would distract the big man at the opportune moment, none the wiser.

Nash couldn't resist. He licked his lips with anticipation of his revenge, chuckling inside that he could magically bring it all off tonight, and relaunch his career into the absolute stratosphere of elite society so much earlier than he had anticipated.

Cleray just had no idea how to bring in the big players to market something like Solaria Femina. And that insistence on maintaining an image of virginal purity for the girls.

Seriously?

Although, perhaps there was something powerful in that thing you could not have.

Perhaps what was needed was to add an older group of such women. Just graduated from the junior varsity, which was only focused on pretty and talented.

Yes, take that and play up the dangerous elements. Bad

girls. Femme fatales. Women stepping out and flaunting their raw sexuality with power and hunger.

There might be no limits whatsoever to what Nash could accomplish, once he convinced Lianearia to put him in charge and let him run things. She was talented as a songwriter and exceptional at recruiting. Let him work on expanding the franchise across a wider audience.

Whoops. There's our captain. Can't get so wrapped up in ourselves that we lose the boy, or let him see us.

Nash watched the lad walk purposefully across that tiny space at the front of the stage that wasn't overly crowded with dancing girls.

Where is he going? Oh, of course. To see his employer.

How delightfully perfect!

Nash moved after the man like a predator sliding through high grass.

Watched Tarasicodissa approach the man guarding the rear of the facility and exchange pleasantries. Obviously, Lianearia had left him on the guest list, because Tarasicodissa was quickly ushered through the door and into the back of the club.

Nash paused just long enough to reach around and touch the stun pistol tucked into the back of his belt, confirming that he could get at it quickly enough.

And now, my dears, let us have a private conversation. Of course, off-site, but don't worry, I brought transport. And if you don't want to go, I'll just have to shoot you and have one of Arturious's men pick you up and bring you along.

At last.

[24]
KYRIAKI

She had learned the art of being unseen in a crowd when she was younger. Kyriaki had never been the most beautiful girl in her class. Or the smartest. Or the most athletic. Tallest. Shortest.

Perhaps none of the –est options.

Unless you counted ambition. Then she probably was the hungriest. The one driven the hardest. It got her into the burgundy and white.

It got her here.

But she was functionally invisible now, watching people come and go. She knew Cleray was here. And she had spotted Tarasicodissa and Hall, reclining in a booth to one side. They had a good view of the dance floor and the stage, but the lights on the rest of the club would obscure her, although she doubted either man would remember what she looked like after their one, brief encounter.

Still, best not to take any chances. She could observe the man in his natural condition. See who he met with. What choices he made.

What made Valentinian Tarasicodissa tick.

She watched him banter with Hall for a few minutes, sipping beer like neither of them had a care in the world.

Like the White Hats weren't always watching you…

Her target rose and made his way down front. Presumably visiting the head.

Kyriaki moved to keep both men in view, just another girl in this club checking out the fresh meat.

As if.

Her new spot was closer to the door at the rear of the club, across the dance floor from the main bar. It kept her distant and ill-defined, while letting her watch.

Someone else moved in such a way that he seemed to be shadowing Tarasicodissa. The flickering lights were enough to obscure the stranger's face, but his movement was out of synch with the rest of the bar, so he stood out to her like a dandelion in a rose bush.

Strobes lit the dance floor as a new song started.

Past the spike of blindness, Kyriaki recognized the man stalking Valentinian.

Nash Bogomelous.

How utterly perfect.

She smiled. Checked around the man for the bodyguards she would have expected. Saw none.

Kyriaki couldn't decide if that made things better or worse.

Was a man like Nash more dangerous without backup, when he might be desperate, or with help, when he could play the bully?

Still, it let her get closer to the man that she might have, otherwise. He was too focused on Valentinian to pay much attention to her.

Kyriaki found a good spot and watched.

Valentinian emerged from the restrooms and began to head across the base of the stage towards her. But more importantly, towards the door to the rear where Cleray waited with her girls.

Probably checking in with the woman. Possibly sneaking a chance to see the girls in some state of indecent nudity as they got into their costumes. Kyriaki growled under her breath.

The bouncer by the door let the man through grumpily, after making a performance out of checking the list of acceptable names. Kyriaki was nearly annoyed on behalf of Valentinian, but the man seemed rather mellow, considering what she had read in his file.

She turned her attention back to Nash, just in time to see the man lift his jacket and uncover a stun pistol in a rear holster.

Kyriaki really didn't like the look in the man's eyes as he started after Valentinian. That was the sort of face a man made when he was about to cause a ruckus. Considering the interpersonal dynamics at play, Kyriaki was away from the column that had been mock-supporting her weight and moving after Nash as quickly as she could thread through the crowd.

Her small stature worked against her here. The mob was heavier, the closer she got to the dance floor.

She watched Nash approach the bouncer and draw his stun pistol from under his coat. The man's expression was turned away from her, but the smile on the bouncer's face spoke volumes about the ambush that was about to happen.

Briefly, she considered drawing her own stun pistol, but the range was too great, and the crowd too heavy to get a sure shot off.

And from here, she would just cause the rabbits to scatter. Right at the moment she had them all in one trap.

Kyriaki pushed, knowing she would be too late to get there before whatever confrontation happened.

Nash lacking bodyguards left her cold. The back of her mind added the pieces together and decided that he had left them nearby, and was just waiting his chance to pull his own ambush on Cleray and her captain.

She muttered one of the foulest obscenities she knew and elbowed a tall blond out of the way hard enough that the woman might be peeing blood tomorrow.

Kyriaki didn't wait around long enough to ask.

[25]

VALENTINIAN

THROUGH THE DOOR, Valentinian felt his humor improving already, but that was just the volume of the music coming down to merely painful thresholds from what it had been outside.

There was a reason he liked quiet dives. Or the ones with occasional jazz bands. Less of an audible assault.

The back of the club almost felt like a movie set, with half the walls just raw metal beams that had been painted, rather than wood and finish like the front. Down the hallway, as he had been directed, Valentinian turned left at the first juncture and went through a doorway into a larger space.

If it had been smaller, he would have called it a Green Room, but it was big enough to hold all of Solaria Femina right now. Not just the nine girls, but the rest of the support staff that was on site, so about fifteen people.

And it wasn't even that crowded in here.

Many of the girls saw him and smiled. A few waved.

Madame Cleray was talking to Fahrettin about something when he entered. She turned his direction with an enormous scowl on her face that only slightly lessened when she saw who was causing the interruption.

"Ah, Captain Tarasicodissa," she said, causing Valentinian to double-take.

Captain Tarasicodissa was his father. Still, she was talking to him. And at least mildly happy that he was here, if the complicated play of emotions in her eyes was any hint.

It had only been an instant, but Arcades was all about reading a person's soul in that pulse when they first spied their seventh card, the Build card always dealt face down. To know if they've built their arcade, or are frantically calculating the final round of betting and whether they can stay in or drop out.

Lianearia Cleray had drawn a run of Stones, and not even across the colors. Maybe she could win if she pushed her bluff hard enough and everything fell apart for everyone else?

What the hell had he done to piss this woman off?

Valentinian rolled quickly backwards over the last three days in his head as he advanced to shake her hand, but nothing jumped out as a trigger that he should watch his kidneys for a knife. Maybe he had just timed it to arrive on the heels of bad news?

"I won't stay long," Valentinian smiled as brightly as he could. "Just wanted to thank you for the invitation and let you know Dave and I are out front if you needed us to do anything or run back to the ship for something you forgot."

Her face cracked as she numbly shook his hand. It was like an avalanche spalling off the front of the mountain, being replaced by a wholly different woman, this one smiling.

Either she had suddenly remembered to put on her Valentinian face for lying, or whatever it was wasn't his fault.

Valentinian wasn't going to stay long enough to press the issue.

"Thank you," she said neutrally. "It has been helpful, having the two of you around,"

Weird, but sure. Maybe the stress of opening night was making the woman apocalyptic, but that sure sounded like the sort of brush off he had used a few times, when some woman looked like she wanted him to *settle down and get a real job*, as opposed to doing what he loved.

"Ma'am," he nodded. He turned to the rest of the troupe. "Good luck."

Valentinian turned and took a step before he registered that there was someone standing in the doorway.

And holding a stunner pointed right at his chest.

"Going somewhere, Captain Tarasicodissa?"

Nash? Her old partner?

Here?

Shit.

"Nash?" Madame Cleray's voice sounded almost as surprised as Valentinian felt. "What are you doing?"

No. She was honestly surprised. Valentinian was just pissed.

Talk about your rookie mistakes. They didn't come much worse.

He should have expected this. Shouldn't have assumed Nash would take a night off to scout them before moving

Should have brought Dave. Nothing would have snuck up on the big guy.

"Why, I've come to have a chat, darling," Nash oozed false *bonhomie* over his words, like cream that had gone bad. "Don't do anything stupid, boy."

That last a threat to Valentinian as he tensed.

The shock pistol was tucked in under his jacket where he could never get to it in time to be useful.

At least that was a stunner the man held, and not anything heavier. Maybe he did just want to talk, but

Valentinian couldn't imagine anything Nash wanted to say that was worth hearing. There would still be a ration of pain later, most likely.

Unless the man just wanted to get them someplace private before he got lethal. Too many witnesses here, like he had expected. Or maybe there were more people in on it than he or Cleray had expected.

"There is nothing to talk about, Nash," Madame Cleray's voice was cruelty itself, distilled down to a fine brandy and served mulled. "We're no longer in business together, so you are free to do whatever it is men like you do when they're alone."

Valentinian blinked hard at the words, and they weren't even aimed at him.

Nash turned nearly purple, with some bizarre alchemy of rage and embarrassment.

"We'll just see about that," the man snarled.

He reached into a pants pocket and pulled out his card-reader, thumbing it live.

"Arturious," he said conversationally. "Could you join me in the back room?"

Yup. Bringing friends. This conversation just got a whole lot less friendly. It was like a storm front suddenly passing with a rain squall.

Somewhere, a door opened loudly. Possibly the back door where the bus had dropped Madame Cleray and the girls off earlier. Heavy feet slapping loudly on the concrete floors.

Half a dozen men suddenly appeared behind Nash. Big men.

Valentinian didn't recognize any faces, but there was no doubting their purpose.

More bully-boys. The same sort that had nearly kicked his ass back on Dominion Prime. Except Dave wasn't here to bail him out this time. And two of them also had stunners.

Charmingly, Nash turned enough of his attention to Kostantina and Fahrettin.

"The show must go on," he instructed them, adding a cruel and vengeful edge to his voice. "I'll have Lianearia back to you after your performance, hopefully none the worse for wear. You will take charge of the girls and make this first show memorable. Am I understood?"

Valentinian heard silence.

"I am not trifling here," Nash roared. "Am I understood?"

Somewhere behind him, Valentinian caught voices mixing curses with assents. Possibly some weeping.

"Good," Nash turned his gaze back to Valentinian. The pistol had never wavered. "I'm just going to make this easier on everyone."

And the bastard shot him.

[26]
KYRIAKI

"I NEED TO SEE LIANEARIA CLERAY," Kyriaki repeated. "It's urgent."

"Sorry, lady," the bouncer with the clipboard said. "You ain't on the list."

"You let me back there earlier," she tried a different tack.

"You were with her then," the man smiled cruelly.

"Will one of you at least go get her for me?" Kyriaki asked. "Let her know I'd like to talk to her?"

"No," the bouncer was smug now. "You call her yourself and she'll come up. But we've got instructions. Go away."

There was one card left to play at this point, and she was debating it when the screams started. They were faint, but recognizable, even through the heavy door.

Terror. Possibly the sound of beamfire as well, but it was hard to tell over the sound of the music.

The four bouncers heard it. That much was obvious from the grimaces that passed over their faces. The set of shoulders suddenly hunching forward.

Whatever was happening back there, they had at least

expected trouble. And been told to stay out of it. Not one of them so much as glanced back.

Kyriaki growled and reached for her card-reader and her stun pistol.

Suddenly, the four of them were armed as well. Two shock rods and a pair of shock pistols appeared.

Standoff.

"I have my instructions," the lead bouncer said. "It's not worth getting fired over."

She activated her card-reader carefully and turned it to show her identcard to the man.

"Dominion Internal Security. Is it worth going to prison?" she asked.

From the looks on at least two of them, they already knew what the inside of a jail cell smelled like. But nobody wavered.

And she couldn't take on four of them.

The screams had peaked and were starting to recede now. And you had to be this close to the door to hear them, so most of the crowd would be ignorant, regardless.

Kyriaki set her jaw. She would shoot the leader, the one holding one of the shock pistols, and then try to use the nearer goon with the rod as cover while she tried to get through them.

Nash was up to no good. Possibly Cleray had set him up. And Valentinian.

Maybe the woman was a black widow, and using the whole thing as cover to clear decks. She had looked that dangerous.

The bouncers tensed as well.

"I don't think you understand," a new voice suddenly called out. "We're going through that door. Your only choice now is if we go around you, or over your bodies."

Kyriaki slid a little sideways so she could glance back as the bouncers suddenly reacted to something behind her.

Dave Hall stood there.

Big. Angry. As dangerous as a Kodiak roused mid-winter.

The two with shock pistols ignored her and aimed at the sudden intruder.

Dave Hall's next words would haunt her nightmares for years.

"What?" he asked in a cruel voice. "You don't think I can't take all four of you at once?"

She watched him snap his right hand out and down suddenly.

A sword appeared in it, telescoping out from a handle.

She recognized the style of grip, even if the blade part was a flattened tube of metal sections rather than a sharpened steel blade.

Caelon grip. The Dominator's Assault Cavalry shock troops. The most dangerous, most lethal force in the galaxy.

And she suddenly knew she was seeing the assassin himself. Up close and deadly.

The bouncers knew it as well. Something about the man's casual stance conveyed to them of Hall's utter conviction that he would kill four men before they could even blink, and feel no more remorse than plucking a chicken for dinner.

"White Hats," she growled loudly at the suddenly-shaken men. "Stand aside."

They did this time.

Kyriaki burst through the door with Hall on her heels. The screaming was turning into sobs now, so she followed that sound.

Big room. Filled with frantic women.

Kyriaki held up her badge card and turned to the oldest woman.

"What happened?" she demanded.

This woman had seen worse in her life. She swallowed once and visibly calmed herself.

"Nash was here," she said. "Shot Lianearia and Valentinian with stunners. Took them out the back door. They're gone."

Kyriaki pivoted, but Hall was already moving, so she fell into his wake.

He had nothing more than that pseudo-sword, and somehow she felt out-gunned here.

But so would Nash and his friends.

Hall moved without hesitation. His long legs gave him an edge, so Kyriaki put her head down and concentrated on speed. Hall would kill anything they passed that needed killing.

Of that, she had no doubts.

Out the back door, a van was just pulling out of the alleyway. She moved around a suddenly-still Hall and saw Nash smiling at her from the rear window.

"Now what?" Hall rumbled.

"Now we find out who else knew," Kyriaki said. "And get them to talk."

"Agreed," Hall said in a voice that made her shiver.

Kyriaki had always thought she was the hardest person she knew.

Yesterday, that had still been the truth.

The tall man turned with purpose and strode back into the building. She fell into his wake. It didn't help that Hall was more than an entire head taller than she was, and possibly twice as broad, and probably outweighed her by double.

Besides that, he was a stone killer.

Back inside, the bouncers had followed them deeper into the building. Two of them, anyway. The others were probably still keeping the riffraff out.

"Where's the manager?" Hall asked the leader in a voice so quiet that the man had to lean forward to hear it.

Death probably sounded like that, when he came for you with his own clipboard.

"I'm the owner," another voice rang out. "What seems to be going on here?"

Kyriaki was a strong woman. She worked out regularly with all the machines and ran good distances to stay in peak shape.

She could have never done this.

Hall reached out with his left hand, the one not holding the sword, and caught the newcomer by the throat. It helped that the man was Kyriaki's rough height and size. His bald head gleamed with sudden sweat.

Dave Hall lifted the man bodily off the ground by his jawbone, holding him aloft until the tiny man's feet swung like a child's.

"You're going to tell me where they took my captain," Hall quietly instructed the man.

Death was probably jealous of that voice as well.

One of the bouncers took a half-step forward, and stopped when Hall's sword suddenly came up and centered on his face. Hall never took his eyes off the tiny man he was holding.

"What makes you think…?"

The rest of the words were squeezed back down the man's throat by Hall's grip, suddenly tightening just enough to get his attention.

"You will listen to me," Hall said in a quiet voice. A scary one. "I already have a Death Warrant on my head, so killing you won't put me in hell any longer than I was already facing. You can talk, or I can ask someone else when you're dead. Do you understand me?"

Even the sobs from the girls fell silent. Kyriaki was sure everyone but her had forgotten to even breathe.

Death Warrant.

Nothing like that had come up when she had inspected *Longshot Hypothesis* and run all their identcards that day. Including Dave Hall.

Or whatever his name really was.

She had fallen for the same shell game as everyone else, watching Valentinian and ignoring his first mate.

The man who had, oh by the way, joined the vessel on Dominion Prime, apparently right after he had assassinated the Dominator.

For a moment, she considered shooting the killer and taking him in. Leaving Valentinian and Cleray to their fates. But that wasn't why she had put on the white beret. She was a cop, not an executioner.

Regardless of how much Hall deserved it.

She could always shoot him later.

The man in Hall's grip gurgled once. Possibly Hall making a point.

"I'll talk," the man whispered hoarsely. "It wasn't supposed to happen like this at all."

Hall lowered the man to the ground delicately, like an antique vase. That display of pure strength was almost more frightening than the rage it took to lift him in the first place.

Except that it hadn't been rage. Dave Hall really was that strong.

Kyriaki moved to watch the bouncers, but they were hollow now, in complete shock.

Seizing her moment, she stripped the men of their pistols. They didn't even resist her at this point.

"Nash wanted to get back together with Lianearia," the old man said, carefully rubbing the skin of his neck. "Was going to negotiate a new deal, after the old one fell apart. I warned him that contracts were better than intimidation, but he never listens to anyone but himself."

"Where are they?" Hall asked in a voice that only sounded friendly when you had heard the alternative earlier.

"He has an office downtown," the man said. "I have the address in my card-reader."

He started to reach for his pocket and froze like a rabbit when Hall tensed. He moved much more cautiously, in an elaborate pantomime, withdrawing it and bringing it live.

"Here," he turned it around for them to read.

"Good enough," Hall said after a moment. "I need the keys to your vehicle."

"What?" the man's anger suddenly bubbled back to the surface.

Kyriaki stepped close enough to get the owner's attention. She showed him her own identcard.

"This is a criminal investigation, citizen," she said simply. "You can assist it or become an accessory to the crimes I have already witnessed here. Your choice."

Having a giant killer like Hall handy did wonders to compel obedience. The manager pulled a key ring from his front pocket and handed it to her without a word.

"Bartholomew," the man said over his shoulder. "Show her where you parked it."

Hall surprised her by ignoring the owner and following the lead bouncer without a single glance back. Kyriaki followed, giving Dave the keys.

Back out into the alley, they walked around a corner to a private parking lot, where Bartholomew approached a sports car, an actual land vehicle that ran on black tires.

"Thank you," Hall said to the man as he pressed a button and the vehicle's alarm system sent back a welcoming chirp.

Bartholomew left like he had been shot out of a cannon.

Hall turned to study her. He still had his sword. She had her stunner.

They were alone in the lot.

It wasn't remotely a fair fight, if the man wanted to kill her. And they both knew it.

"You're the assassin I've been hunting since Dominion Prime," she said simply.

Hall surprised her by shrugging eloquently.

"That, Inspector, is a very philosophical topic to attempt," he said in a voice that sounded more like a college professor than a Caelon trooper. "In some ways, you are correct. In others, you are not."

"How is it possible to be both?" she demanded. "You killed the Dominator. And would have completely escaped justice, but for sheerest luck."

Hall stared at her for a long moment. Made some mental calculation.

"Because I was the Dominator, Inspector," he said finally. "I woke up one morning after twenty-some years and decided I wanted more out of life, so I faked my own assassination, as they subsequently termed it. Vanished into the night, leaving only a letter to my wife and another to the head of the Solar Party. Told them I was done and wasn't coming back."

Kyriaki sucked a hard breath in. His raw emotions were shallow enough that she could detect the truth of the words.

"Does Valentinian know?" she finally demanded, unsure of her own emotions right now.

"He does not," Hall admitted. "Nobody does but my wife, and perhaps a few dozen officials on Dominion Prime. And now you."

She could take the man in. And prove his story one way or the other. Dave Hall would be executed for it.

She would be a hero.

And Nash would get away with whatever evil he had planned for Valentinian and Cleray.

Kyriaki really didn't understand her emotional reaction to Tarasicodissa. The way he smelled different, when she had gotten too close to the man. The urge to rescue him now, when she could just call the authorities and let them deal with the situation in their own way.

Bad boys were not her thing.

And yet, nobody had ever been able to make anything stick on Tarasicodissa. Even getting kicked out of the Gymnasia Dominia had all the hallmarks of a cover-up by others.

"I only ask you this," Hall continued as he watched her, a mongoose eyeing a cobra. "Let me rescue Valentinian. Then you can take me in."

She teetered. Watched the man open the driver's door to the car and reset the seat all the way back before he tried to get in.

Could not make up her mind.

Kyriaki sprinted to the far side of the car and pulled the door open, throwing herself into the passenger seat before she had a chance to change her mind.

"We'll talk," she said.

[27]

DAVE

He had enjoyed being Dave Hall. That man had none of the issues facing him that a long-time Dominator had faced. He could simply travel the galaxy and see new things, learning how to be a spacer from a man with his own skeletons and issues to deal with.

Dave glanced over at the woman beside him. She reminded him of Euphrosyne, his daughter back home on Dominion Prime.

Or wherever she would end up in the aftermath of a new Tournament of Domination.

Dave tried to feel some level of guilt at just chucking his life out the window and walking into the night, but it was like a missing tooth in his mouth.

Hollow.

Euphrosyne would land on her feet. Just as her mother would. Praetextatus was already making his way as a young Caelon officer, following in his father's footprints rather than joining the Armada.

It tickled Dave that his son and Valentinian might have

met and possibly been friends, had the boy sought a naval career.

The car was over-powered for its weight. Electric motors in all four wheels delivered enough power to make driving at this speed a hazardous undertaking, but Dave was in a hurry and let his anger steer his reflexes.

The White Hat beside him had buckled herself in tight and still had a foot braced on the dash and a hand on the ceiling. But then, it wasn't like Dave cared what condition he left the man's car in when he was done.

Hell, if it was possible, he would have rammed Nash's van and taken his chances in the fracas immediately afterward, but too much time had probably passed, even for a Thursday night.

A red light stopped him long enough to check the map on his card-reader against his memory. Six blocks up and three over. Corporate tower district.

"Why are you doing this?" Inspector Kyriaki Apokapes asked quietly from the seat.

"This?" Dave answered in that distant, lethal voice. "Because I warned Nash the first time. He didn't listen."

"No, I meant the disguise," she pursued the topic. "Why the elaborate charade and staging your own death?"

"You cannot retire from that job, Inspector," Dave said simply. "You die in office. Either by your own hand, or when a challenger convinces the Solar Party that you need to be deposed and a new Tournament of Domination is called. I would have changed that, if I could. But it was bigger than me."

"And Valentinian?" she faced him as he waited for the light.

"All my research suggested he would be the perfect tool to confuse any investigation, Inspector. A man with a shadowy past that would distract you from looking at anything else," Dave glanced over and grinned at her. "Worked, didn't it?"

"Yes," she conceded in a voice that couldn't decide if it wanted to be triumphant or angry. "But why not let Nash keep him? You could have gotten completely away and nobody would have been the wiser."

"Valentinian is in danger because I put him there," Dave growled as the light turned green.

The car leapt like a panther on fresh spoor. The girl fell quiet as the car raced silently through the darkness.

Dave found the building. A low rise in a seedier part of downtown, butting up against a series of warehouses.

Rather than scream into an ambush, Dave circled the block.

There were lights on in a single office on the fourth floor, and most of the seventh.

Dave found an alley and parked the car in a no parking zone, hoping it at least got ticketed, if not towed. He would never set foot in that bar again to properly discuss the owner's participation in all this, so he settled for pettiness.

If it wouldn't have caused so much noise, he would have shattered the windshield with his sword. That sort of thing wasn't supposed to be possible, but Dave was willing to experiment, right now.

He exited. The girl joined him.

"I could call the authorities," she suggested weakly.

"This is Tartarus City, Inspector," Dave laughed at her. "Chances are we get arrested for stealing the car before they ever get around to investigating a kidnapping report. Nash would have set things up ahead of time."

She grunted rather than reply.

Dave moved instead.

"So how do we approach this?" she finally asked as they jogged quickly along the alley and crossed the street to stand next to their target. It was obvious the young woman viewed herselr as his partner, and not his parole officer.

"You're going in the front door," Dave said. "Fourth floor. Suite six. Your job will be to arrest all of them."

"Just like that?" she turned angry eyes on him. "What will you be doing?"

"Coming in the window and killing everything that moves," Dave said simply, letting is anger talk now.

"How?" she demanded in an angry whisper.

"Watch me, Inspector," Dave said implacably.

Dave had the sword stowed already in the thigh holster. He took three fast steps and leapt up against the building, planting his right foot against the stone and thrusting upwards until he caught the bottom of a fire escape, nearly five meters off the ground.

Below him, Inspector Kyriaki Apokapes watched with her mouth open, until she remembered to close it and turned to find the front of the building.

Dave smiled and pulled himself up onto the first level.

Only the very best are ever allowed wear the Caelon armor.

Of those, Dave Hall had been the greatest.

[28]
KYRIAKI

BLOOD AND MARTYRS. The man had pogoed himself off the building and caught the bottom of the metal rack overhead. Kyriaki had never heard of someone with that sort of agility. And worse, the man was old enough to be her father.

What must he have been like as a young Dominator?

No wonder so many of their galactic neighbors slept uneasily.

Kyriaki caught her breath and drew her stun pistol, holding it close to her side as she approached the front of the building. It was late in the day, but the season was still summer, so the sun had only just set.

There were four doors across the front of the building. A security guard was in the process of locking the middle one when she approached and pulled one he hadn't gotten to.

"Building's closed, ma'am," he said politely.

She pulled her card-reader and showed him her identcard. Watched him blanch in shock and catch his breath.

If Dave Hall could be her father, this man could be her grandsire, seven or eight decades old and built like a bean pole. Kyriaki thought she might outweigh the man, in spite of him being nearly Dave's height.

"Official investigation," Kyriaki said as firmly as she could.

White Hats scared everyone. It was a hammer in her hands as often as it was a dirk, but it worked in her favor right now.

"What can I do?" the man asked in a frightened voice.

"Nothing," Kyriaki informed him sternly. "Lock these doors and you can continue your rounds, but stay out of my way. Or better, do you have a place you can hide?"

"Hide, ma'am?" He was scared now.

"It's going to get ugly," Kyriaki replied. "Find a quiet place and lock yourself in for the next hour. You'll know when it is safe to emerge."

"Yes, ma'am." The man fled, leaving her in charge of the lobby.

She considered the elevators, but wanted to sneak up on Nash. Walking into a trap if the man had left someone to watch on the fourth floor wouldn't help.

Kyriaki found the front stairwell and marked the location in her mind. Then she went and found the rear one, cracking the door and ascending in as much silence as she could manage in the harsh whiteness.

Nobody was in the shaft as she got to the fourth floor, so she cracked the door and peeked out into a carpeted hallway. Nobody in sight.

Kyriaki slipped out of the stairwell behind her pistol and looked for a nearby door.

Number eleven. Down the hallway, closer to the turn, number ten.

She moved like a ghost, thinking about all the times she had found it necessary to just kick in a door at the head of a column of armed troops.

Tonight, she would need subtle. She slithered up to the corner and moved like a glacier as she peeked.

Nobody in sight.

Stupid.

Nash should have left at least one man in the hallway, to guard against someone doing exactly what she was up to.

But Nash was a punk, and had hired more punks. She was a cop. Dave Hall was a renegade Caelon, a killer.

And quite possibly her sovereign lord in hiding.

Still, if these people wanted to make mistakes, who was she to correct them before it became time? Just in case, she checked for cameras, but nothing was evident.

Good enough.

She moved around the corner, ready to shoot anything that moved. That was the advantage of a stunner over anything more dangerous. You had the chance to apologize later if you made a mistake.

Not that she was expecting anything tonight, but some accountant might have chosen to work late, and then suddenly walked into a firefight.

Number six. Simple internal door. Probably pseudo-wood grain over a plascore.

Whoops.

Kyriaki started to brace her weight for a kick, and then stopped and wondered.

How stupid might these people really be?

Carefully, she rested her hand on the brass handle. Maybe she imagined it, but the metal felt warm, like maybe it hadn't been opened all that long ago.

She gripped it and put just enough pressure on the metal to see that it would turn.

Really, you didn't even lock it?

Or was that the trap? Open the door and step in, as the man on the other side shot you in the chest?

That sounded more like Axarnashalic Bogomelous.

Still, two can play.

Kyriaki turned the handle completely and shoved the door hard, stepping back out of the way to hide behind the frame.

Beam fire blistered the far wall and threatened to light small fires across from her.

Bastards weren't even using shock pistols, but had brought out the flamers. Shortly, the fire alarms would probably start to douse the floor in water, if the wallpaper caught, but she didn't feel like giving them a chance.

Kyriaki reached around the doorframe with her stunner and fired it as fast as she could pull the trigger. Snap. Snap. Snap.

Withdraw as a beam licked at the frame, just missing her arm.

She squatted and did the same thing from knee height, chancing a glance around the corner.

One man already falling, a flamer dropping from his hands. Two more bouncers suddenly scrambling for cover. Kyriaki managed to wing one as he got behind an unused desk. It wouldn't be enough to take him down, from the cursing as his arm went numb, but it would help.

She jumped back behind the door frame, wishing she had a stun grenade right now. And hoping that they didn't.

If this went too long, they might flank her. Either a door might open into another office, or someone might remember that all walls in a tower like this were wood frames covered over with gypsum board.

All you had to do was hammer on it with a chair, in a fire, and you could walk through walls.

More fire bursting on the wall across from her. Angry yells back and forth, muffled by interior walls, furniture, and fright.

Kyriaki stood and reached as high as she could to take another couple of potshots from overhead. She knew where they two men were, if they hadn't moved.

More cursing.

My, such language.

She smiled.

Suddenly, cries of pain. And then silence.

"Inspector, you can come out now," Dave Hall said in a conversational voice. "The threat has been neutralized."

Neutralized? Just like that?

"Inspector?" Hall repeated.

"Yes," she called back, glancing around the frame.

One man down that she had shot. Two more had joined him. At least one of them was dead, from the amount of blood leaking from the man's head.

Kyriaki wasn't squeamish, but she had never seen someone beaten to death with a length of steel tubing. Most deaths were either crimes to be solved well after the fact, and approached professionally, or taken down by a beam weapon. Flamers cauterized wounds.

Hall wasn't even splattered with the blood that covered half his sword.

"All of them?" she was aghast.

"There were only six," Hall smiled at her like a big cat. "And you had them distracted."

She followed him into the inner office, trying to remember to close her suddenly-open mouth.

Only six of them? And he had taken them all out before they even knew what happened?

Two more bouncers were down. It was hard to tell if they were dead without checking vital signs, but they were no longer threats. Valentinian was groggily holding a stun pistol in the general direction of Axarnashalic Bogomelous.

Nash was down on his bottom with his back against a

wall, whimpering mindlessly. From the angle of his right leg, Hall had apparently attempted to sever it with his blunt sword in passing. Had he aimed for the shin instead of the knee, he might have succeeded but she didn't think that the location was accidental. The con man's eyes were all whites and pupils, but that was the pain starting to break through the adrenaline.

Lianearia was unconscious on a sofa along the left hand wall, snoring peacefully.

A window was open at the far end of the space.

Kyriaki was amazed Valentinian was awake.

"How?" she started, before finally running out of words.

Hall grinned at her and triggered a button that collapsed the sword back into a baton barely thirty decimeters long.

"We train for this sort of thing, Inspector," he said simply.

He held the baton out to her to take, apparently surrendering peacefully.

It dawned on Kyriaki, that, as dangerous as she had thought the man was before, Dave Hall was at least an order of magnitude worse. And he was willing to walk to his death with nothing more than her word.

She could arrest him. And be a hero when the man was executed as a traitor to his own crown.

And what justice would that serve?

Worse, what did it say about her own oaths that she was even questioning herself or him right now. What had happened to her?

No, that was the wrong question to ask. Why had arresting Hall been the wrong thing to do?

Because evil would have triumphed.

"Citizen Hall," her words shocked her, but they felt right. "Thank you for your assistance in making this arrest. I think it would be best if you accompanied Captain Tarasicodissa to the hospital, once reinforcements arrive to take charge of the situation. I'll be calling my own forces, and not the local gendarmes."

Hall's eyes held a question as he watched her, brows hooded.

Nobody but her knew the truth, according the man. She could believe it. Nothing could stand against that man if he chose violence.

"You're sure?" he asked one last time, sword still hanging out there for her to take from him.

Kyriaki had never been more sure of anything, including joining the White Hats in the first place.

"I am."

EPILOGUE
VALENTINIAN

"WHY ARE WE ENDING THE CONTRACT?" Valentinian heard Dave ask as *Longshot Hypothesis* powered up.

The cargo bay aft was empty, as the girls had weepily packed everything and moved it to shore storage while Lianearia Cleray worked to extend Solaria Femina's run on Tartarus, at the same time looking for a new cargo transport to charter.

"I had a chat with Inspector Apokapes," Valentinian replied in a quiet voice as he touched the collective.

"Kyriaki?" Dave asked in a tone that Valentinian had never heard from the man.

Wistful? And calling her by her first name?

"Kyriaki," Valentinian agreed.

He wasn't sure how he felt about the woman. She had interviewed him in greater detail than even a business deal gone bad leading to a kidnapping warranted. Like she was checking his bonafides. Digging deep into his life.

At the hospital, while he was being checked out, she had specifically told him to get as far away as he possibly could, as fast as a souped-up thing like *Longshot Hypothesis* could run.

"And?" Dave prompted when Valentinian had apparently fallen into thought.

"Nash won't be a problem," Valentinian finally said. "But I don't think we'll avoid serious scrutiny from Kyriaki's friends if we stay."

"The White Hats?" Dave seemed surprised.

"The Dominion," Valentinian corrected him.

"Meaning?"

"I was coherent enough to see you come through that window, Dave," Valentinian admitted. "To watch you take out all of them before they even knew what happened. Plus Kyriaki told me about how you got up onto the fire escape."

"I see," Dave fell silent.

Valentinian brought power to the collective and his ship poised, ever so briefly before she leapt into the night sky above Tartarus City.

"And?" Dave prompted again into the silence.

"If I don't ever ask the wrong questions, then when the White Hats eventually put me under a truth serum later, I can't tell them anything about you," Valentinian said, almost angry at himself. "So don't tell me anything more than I already know, okay?"

Like how you managed to kill the best-protected man in the galaxy.

Valentinian no longer doubted that Dave Hall was deadly enough to have done the job. Nash and his friends had been about as dangerous as newborn kittens.

"Oh," Dave finally said, so apparently he understood. "Gotcha."

Valentinian nodded gratefully at the man as the ship accelerated into the night sky.

"So now what?" Dave finally asked as they got to a high altitude.

Valentinian wondered where his own words had gone,

but he could answer a direct question, even if he couldn't formulate any better response ahead of time.

"So now I think it would be better if we were maybe beyond the immediate, legal reach of the White Hats for a while," Valentinian said, finally looking at his first mate directly. "They're not ever going to stop looking for you, are they?"

Dave surprised him by shrugging.

"Kyriaki could have taken me in," he said simply. "But she let me, us, go. Maybe she'll cover things up enough. We're just a pair of spacers that got in over our heads, right?"

Valentinian laughed and felt the knot between his shoulder blades finally loosen.

"Over our heads, yeah," he said.

He understood that feeling.

But Dave Hall had chosen to come and rescue him when he could have just disappeared into the night. That made twice he owed the man.

This would pay back one of them, getting out to at least Laurentia for a time, if not all the way into Wildspace.

Maybe the White Hats would forget about them.

And cows might discover FTL.

Blaze Ward writes science fiction in the Alexandria Station universe (Jessica Keller, The Science Officer, The Story Road, etc.) as well as several other science fiction universes, such as Star Dragon, the Collective, and more. He also writes odd bits of high fantasy with swords and orcs. In addition, he is the Editor and Publisher of *Boundary Shock Quarterly Magazine*. You can find out more at his website www.blazeward.com, as well as Facebook, Goodreads, and other places.

Blaze's works are available as ebooks, paper, and audio, and can be found at a variety of online vendors. His newsletter comes out monthly, and you can also follow his blog on his website. He really enjoys interacting with fans, and looks forward to any and all questions—even ones about his books!

Never miss a release!
If you'd like to be notified of new releases, sign up for my newsletter.

I will never spam you or use your email for nefarious purposes. You can also unsubscribe at any time.

http://www.blazeward.com/newsletter/

Connect with Blaze!

Web: www.blazeward.com
Boundary Shock Quarterly (BSQ):
https://www.boundaryshockquarterly.com/

facebook.com/KRPBlaze

goodreads.com/Blaze_Ward

ABOUT KNOTTED ROAD PRESS

Knotted Road Press fiction specializes in dynamic writing set in mysterious, exotic locations.

Knotted Road Press non-fiction publishes autobiographies, business books, cookbooks, and how-to books with unique voices.

Knotted Road Press creates DRM-free ebooks as well as high-quality print books for readers around the world.

With authors in a variety of genres including literary, poetry, mystery, fantasy, and science fiction, Knotted Road Press has something for everyone.

Knotted Road Press
www.KnottedRoadPress.com